Menu For Murder

WITHDRAWN

L. A. Keller

Published by Lacoursiere Publishing

ISBN-13:978-0-9961487-1-9
ISBN-10:099614871X

DEDICATION

To my Mom, who has always believed that
anything I wanted to do was possible and is the most
amazing woman I have ever met.

ACKNOWLEDGMENTS

I would like to thank my sister, Laura, for being my very first reader. For being the one person I knew would give me honest feedback and who probably knows me better than I know myself. Thank you to my partner, Raymond, who pushed me to keep working on the book and helped me work through scenes whenever the words wouldn't come.

To Julie, who was the inspiration for the character of Jayne. Thank you for being the best friend ever and for the crazy times we've shared over the years – some of which might have been included in this novel or may pop up in the next one.

To my "Goddesses", Diann and Philo, who have listened to my complaints, woes and successes over miles of hiking trails, and a few glasses of wine.

Thank you to the wildly talented, Debbie Gioia, who jumped in to design my book cover. I couldn't have done it without your help.

Thank you to my wonderful critique group who kept me motivated and on track.

CHAPTER ONE

"Jayne, run these drinks out and please don't spill any this time."

"Hurry up and take this tray of appetizers to the guests before they get cold."

"Girl, bring me the dirty wine glasses and try not to break any on the way to the kitchen."

That's me they're ordering around, Jayne Stanford, server not so extraordinaire. I was asked—actually required— by my boss at Wild Bronco Steakhouse, to work a private cocktail party tonight hosted at the home of the mayor of our southwestern Arizona town. Even though my manager knew I rebuffed the mayor's advances on more than one occasion,

I either needed to work the party or look for another job. When your eyes are bigger than your budget, you don't pass up the opportunity for a few extra dollars.

I love my job at the restaurant but the guests at this party were enough to make me want to pull my hair out, strand by curly strand. If one more person calls me girl, snaps his fingers or whistles for me to bring his drink, I might have to use this fork for something other than what it was intended.

I recognized some of the most affluent and distinguished Cave Creek, Arizona businesspeople as I dashed back and forth with round after round of cocktails. I also noticed an alarming number of fresh-faced females floating about. I had to wonder if a sorority bus had dropped them off at the wrong party. Not that I was more than a few years older, but in my waitress outfit I was feeling a smidge inadequate in comparison.

The clock finally chimed midnight as I hauled the last of the Baccarat glassware from the dimly lit flagstone patio into the mayor's gourmet kitchen. My aching back gave a last spasm in relief to see the guests start to drift away, and I intended to follow close behind them. I picked up my pace anxious to bring this night to an end and hurry home to my perpetually hungry cat and the home shopping channel.

Unfortunately for me, or maybe for the guests, this

evening had turned out to be forty people who all expected a level of service way beyond my capacity. With only one caterer, one bartender and me as the lone server, I needed wings to fly from kitchen to patio. In my short career, I had never seen people gobble up free food faster than this group. I felt as drained as the empty wineglasses. Sweat plastered my shirt to my back and, with each step, I counted the bones in my feet.

If that wasn't bad enough, I still felt the embarrassment the mayor caused me earlier in the evening. He made quite a spectacle of me before his guests as I served a tray of appetizers.

I shuddered at the memory, recalling the expectant looks on the faces as the mayor said, "Jayne, I've been bragging about your unique memory to my guests all evening." He rested a beefy hand on my lower back. "Tell my guests what I ordered when I was at the restaurant last month. No pressure, my dear, but I've got a hefty bet riding on this." He took the tray from my hands and set it on a nearby table.

My chest tightened momentarily and a volcano of heat exploded up my neck, on display for the entertainment of the mayor's guests. My mind shut down. Nothing, nada, nil. Ten sets of eyes bore into me, waiting for me to perform like a trained circus elephant. The mayor pressed his body closer. I bounced on the balls of my feet.

I sidestepped away from him as nonchalantly as I could, and closed my eyes for a few heartbeats. In my mind, I watched as the days of the calendar rolled back. I saw each of my guests and the plates I served.

"The last thing you ordered was the special of braised bison in a dark ale sauce with pearl onions and baby carrots." I bit my tongue to keep from saying what else I remembered from that night—the mayor's hand on my right butt cheek when he ordered his wine, and later on my left butt cheek as he ordered his dessert.

The small crowd erupted in applause, and my eyes grew wide at the sight of several one hundred dollar bills passed to the mayor.

The mayor grabbed the cash, his diamond cufflinks glittered in the miniature lights hung in the mesquite trees surrounding the patio. "You are magnificent, my pet!" He pulled me to his side again and wrapped his arm around my waist, pressing against me. His claw-like fingers clamped on me like the pinchers of a scorpion and, I imagined, held just as much sting. Hot breath blistered my ear, "I think we should get to know one another better."

Instinctively, I held my breath to avoid breathing in his powerful cologne, swirling around me like a dust storm on an Arizona summer day. My cheeks sizzled and I stifled my desire to gag. I swallowed hard, noticing for the first time the hostess, Tami Lynn Carroll. Her eyes were so dark they might just pierce my skin with their intensity.

Delicately, I extricated myself and retrieved my tray. I vowed to complete this task as expeditiously as I could. The show over, I had guests to serve and dirty dishes to deliver to the housekeeper, who—I will admit—scared me.

Thankfully, the last hour had kept me galloping from guest to guest so I couldn't dwell on why my memory for peculiar details amused everyone but me. Remembering facts about people hadn't done me much good through school but, so far, had kept me working in the restaurant business.

Now, I scouted the perimeter looking for stray plates and overflowing ashtrays, crinkling my nose at the smell of leftover cigars. In the semi-darkness I took a wrong turn and jumped at the forlorn howl of a coyote somewhere nearby, which caused me to trip over my own feet and drop my full tray. The fact that nothing broke provided little consolation, since I had to crawl around on my hands and knees picking up saliva-coated cigar butts, and scout under the shrubs for a missing fork.

With my head halfway under a Palo Verde tree, trying to avoid poking out my eye with one of its thorny branches, I heard raised voices and approaching footsteps crunching on the gravel pathway. Not wanting to get into trouble for dropping the tray, I remained crouched behind the bushes like a timid cottontail rabbit hoping to avoid discovery.

The pungent aroma of cigar smoke tickled my nose and I squelched the urge to sneeze.

"You're overdue on the payment," hissed a voice I recognized as the mayor's.

"I've given you all I can," whined the other man.

"Dig deeper. If I don't get my money by tomorrow, I'll broadcast the truth about you. We'll see how your happy little family feels about that."

"You're killing me," moaned the other man.

The tiny hairs on my arms raised as the tension crackled through the air. I nibbled a cuticle before I remembered dirt crusted my hands.

"Ha, better you than me. Now I must see my other guests off."

With the last comment, heavy footsteps marched away hurriedly, and I risked a peek between the branches. A cigar smokestack trailed in the mayor's wake.

The other man departed with slow shuffling footfalls. I stretched my neck around the edge of the shrub and saw the tall, lanky silhouette of Trent Hayworth, the chairman of the local women's shelter. Rumor had it the construction of the new shelter had stalled recently due to lack of funds. I now knew into whose pocket those funds disappeared, and that helped explain the mansion the mayor occupied on a small-town government salary.

I waited until he was out of sight, brushed myself off, and tiptoed back to the house, all thoughts of the tray forgotten. As I slipped in the back door to the kitchen I ran headlong into Tami Lynn. It was at her request that the soles of my shoes were worn out when I could have been watching the today's special value on television.

I assumed she and the mayor were an "item," but that didn't seem to stop him from flirting with every woman within arm's reach. I don't know why she requested me for this event since I'd waited on her and the mayor only a few times. Maybe it was the fact that they were the only guests from the restaurant I hadn't spilled anything on... yet.

Feeling self-conscious, I looked down at myself, then at the petite Tami Lynn, standing a good four inches below my five-foot-nine-inch frame. The right side of my formerly white shirt was decorated with splotches from three different kinds of red wine; the left side a splash of Pinot Grigio and some kind of mustard-looking stain from the second round of appetizers. Add to that ensemble the dirt which marked the knees of my pants from crawling around in the bushes. Looks like I would have a wild date later on with the stain spray.

Tami Lynn, with her blonde hair perfectly coifed,

balanced delicately in a pair of red-soled shoes, the kind women love to show off. Her skin-tight designer cocktail dress left little to the imagination. Her breasts were pushed so high they almost touched her chin.

She held out an envelope. "You did a surprisingly good job tonight. Here's your pay and a little something extra from me. Make sure you stay and help clean up."

"Thank you so much. I think the party went well," I said temporarily mesmerized by the jewels on her fingers.

"Believe me, the fun is only getting started." With that she gave me a little ta-ta wave with her fingertips and sashayed off to talk to a cluster of Scottsdale princesses who stood gossiping in the corner like ladies-in-waiting for the queen.

I removed my apron, stuffed the envelope in the pocket, and started boxing up the empty wine bottles. Moving with energy I didn't think I had, it only took twenty minutes to finish the cleanup. The mayor's housekeeper loaded the last of the glassware in the industrial-size dishwasher, the bartender evaporated with the remaining liquor, and the caterer packed her van and made a hasty exit. With any luck, I'd be on my sofa with a bowl of buttered popcorn and the television remote in less than thirty minutes.

"Excuse me, ma'am. Where should I put these?" I asked the housekeeper as I held the box of empty wine bottles.

"Go around the back patio to the left. Make sure to put them in the trash cans and not on the ground." She pointed a bony finger in the direction of the back door.

"These can be recycled. Is there a can for that?"

"Hurry up and get out before the boss comes in here. It's not a good idea to hang around like some lost dog looking for a bone. Stay out of the way of trouble and go home." She gave me a push and started turning out lights, limping as she went.

Her demeanor from the start of the evening left no doubt we wouldn't be future best friends, but her abrupt tone startled me. I considered asking what she meant, or if she needed anything else, but something about her gave me the creeps, so I didn't dare.

As I ambled out to the trash cans, I pondered her last comment. Was she calling me a dog, or did she think I deliberately hung around for more money? My conscience wouldn't allow me to throw the glass bottles in the trash so I hauled them around to my car to put them in the trunk. I would take them to the recycling center tomorrow. Unable to navigate lifting up the trunk while holding the heavy box, I set it down and opened the trunk of the car, balancing my purse on the side. It took a few minutes for me to wedge the bulky box inside. I closed the trunk and looked around for my purse. Unless it decided to walk off by itself, or a fashion-conscious owl swooped down and grabbed it, my purse was now locked in the trunk. I was stranded.

Damn it, how did I always manage to complicate my life? For once I would like things to be easy.

The spare key at my apartment rested quietly in its place miles from the mayor's house, so no way would I opt to walk home and back. I already committed the money I made for working this party, so now I would have to spend it on cab fare instead. I guess I would just return the new three-tier, shag-carpeted, kitty condo I ordered for my old rescue cat Bugsy.

Shoulders slumped, I walked back into the house, dragging my feet. The kitchen was deadly quiet and dark except for a small light over the stove.

I jumped as a voice behind me said, "This evening is getting better all the time. I'm pleased to find you're still here."

"Oh, geez. You scared the heck out of me, Mayor McArthur! I was just leaving. Well, actually I locked my keys in the trunk of my car. Can I use your phone to call a cab?" I was chattering with a sudden nervous energy.

"Nonsense. I would be happy to drive you home. But, first, let's have a drink."

"I wouldn't want to inconvenience you or Tami

Lynn." I looked around him to see if she lingered. After overhearing the argument between the mayor and his guest I knew I needed to be as careful as a naked man climbing over a barbed wire fence. Something told me it wasn't a good idea to piss off Tami Lynn. Even if they weren't exclusive.

"Don't worry about Tami, she's passed out somewhere, and all my other guests are gone. Furthermore, one drink won't take that long. I want to get to know you better. I admit to being intrigued by you ever since the first time you waited on me." He walked over to a small side bar in between the kitchen and family room. "What's your poison?"

I caught myself nibbling on a fingernail so I stuffed my hands in my pockets. "I'll just have a diet soda."

Franklin stared at himself in the gold-framed mirror over the bar, smoothed the four strands of hair—which didn't begin to cover the scalp dotted with age spots—and leered at me from his reflection. He selected a crystal cocktail glass, added two ice cubes, a hefty four-finger pour of amber liquid and pressed it into my hand. "You'll enjoy this. It's my best scotch."

I took a small sip. The liquor seared a path all the way down my throat. It tasted like smelly socks.

He sauntered to the ebony leather sofa and plopped his hefty body onto it. Patting the cushion beside him he said,

"Come sit next to me and tell me about yourself."

I remained standing, "Um, there really isn't much to tell."

He patted the sofa again. "I promise I won't bite. I gather you aren't from around here."

Hoping to move things along, I cautiously perched on the edge of the sofa. "I moved here from a small town on the eastern shore just over a year ago."

"You're a long way from home. What brought you to this part of Arizona?"

I would never admit the truth that re-runs of the old television show Bonanza, which I watched as a kid, had been the draw to move west. Cowboys on horses riding the range and looking for a lady to rescue. "Just looking for a change."

"Do you have any family here? Perhaps a husband or a boyfriend?"

"No, it's just me. My mother still lives in Maryland and my father passed away when I was twelve."

"How terribly sad. Was he ill?"

"No, in a boating accident." I never talked to anyone about the day my father died. The memory was burned into me, leaving me branded with the guilt. "I should leave. If it's too much trouble I can call a cab." I stood, hoping to motivate him.

The mayor set his glass on the coffee table with a

loud clink. He stood, and I saw him sway slightly. He took three rapid steps in my direction, and before I could move away, he was all over me like hot fudge on a sundae. He grabbed at the front of my shirt and thrust his other hand into the tangle of my hair, clenching a fistful. Yanking me to him, he plastered his lips on mine trying to force his tongue into my mouth.

Reflexively, I wrenched my head back and, in the process, accidentally flung the cocktail glass across the room where it shattered violently.

"Ewww," was all I could manage.

"Come on, baby. Just one little kiss." He slurred his words, and I felt a drop of spittle hit my face.

"I'd rather kiss the backside of a mule."

"I like it when a girl plays hard to get."

My fingernails were bitten to the stub so I couldn't scratch his face, but I wore my size-nine heavy-duty work shoes. I stomped down as powerfully as I could on his foot, which was just enough to make him release his grip.

"I'm not hard to get. I mean, I'm not playing hard to get. I'll walk home." I reached only as far as the kitchen before he grabbed my shirt from behind.

"That wasn't the least bit nice. But if you want to play rough, I like that, too," he breathed into my hair.

I thrashed about, trying to get free of his grip,

knocking a heavy ceramic platter on the floor where it exploded into dozens of pieces. Dragging him with me, I lunged toward the phone perched on the corner of the marble countertop, but only managed to knock that on the floor as well. His fingers made indentations in my arms as he turned me around and jammed his body against mine. I gagged as I tasted the scotch from his hot breath, and his red-rimmed eyes held the look of a man accustomed to getting what he wanted.

"Please let me go," I begged.

"Don't be so uptight."

He forced his mouth over mine and, letting go of my arms, he pawed at my shirt trying to grab my breasts. I clawed at him, managing a small scratch on his cheek, and tried to get my knee up to his groin, but his weight kept me from moving enough to maneuver into position. My left hand scrambled over the countertop, desperately searching for anything I could use as a weapon. Ignoring the pain as my fingertips sliced across the sharp blade of a paring knife I grabbed it and jabbed it at him, drawing blood from a small puncture to his arm.

He shrieked and took a step back, inspecting his arm as blood started to seep through his designer shirt. This gave me enough room to pull away, and I heard a loud rip as my shirt tore. Suddenly I was free.

I bolted out the back door and dashed around to the front of the house with my feet barely touching the ground. I didn't risk pausing long enough to glance over my shoulder to see if he followed me. Far away, I heard a dog barking, but I was disoriented. It could have been a coyote on the hunt. Fearful he would catch me and force me back into the house, I kicked into a higher gear and sprinted down his driveway.

Forgetting his property was gated, I slid to a stop just before barreling headlong into the metal structure, a sharp pain in my side reminding me my body wasn't accustomed to running anywhere. Apparently, the few extra pounds I'd gained weren't enough to catch the electronic eye and open the gate automatically, so my only option involved climbing over the top. Of course, it's the one time when being an Amazon woman didn't come in handy. I clamored up and was just preparing to drop over the other side when the gate started to open. With half of me hanging over each side, headlights temporarily blinded me. Instinctively, I froze, thinking this is how a prisoner must feel escaping over the fence of a prison.

The passenger-side car door opened. "Get in. I'll drive you home."

I righted myself atop the gate, but made no move to climb down. "I'm not sure that's a good idea, Mayor."

"I'm sorry. I just got carried away. I promise to be on

my best behavior."

I debated my options while perched there above him. Believe him and get a ride home in the sedan of Satan? Start walking in the dark alone with who-knows-what wild desert creatures wandering about looking for their next meal? What were the odds of finding someone who would open their door to me at this hour of the night? My choices were limited, but my knees knocked from our episode only moments before.

I slowly climbed down off the gate and, standing a safe distance away, peered into the barely lit car. I cringed at the kitchen towel wrapped around his arm and seeping a small patch of blood.

He followed my gaze. "It's only a scratch. Fortunately, my housekeeper doesn't leave butcher knives lying about."

"I-I'm sorry," I stammered.

"Do you want a ride or not?"

I thought about it for a moment longer. At almost the same moment I planned to relent and climb in, I caught a glimmer in his eye, which made me step back.

"I overheard you talking to Mr. Hayworth earlier tonight," I blurted out.

"I spoke with all of my guests during the evening. That isn't news worthy."

"I-I heard you threaten him about money."

I backed away from the car as he opened the driver's side door and stepped out. I gathered up my courage. "I know you're blackmailing him."

Mayor McArthur stopped in his tracks, briefly stunned into silence.

He regained his composure in a flash and sneered at me. "You're imagining things. What do you think you heard?"

"I'll tell the police you're blackmailing Trent Hayworth to steal from the Women's Shelter fund." My words sounded brave, but the quaver in my voice betrayed me.

Even in the dark of the night, I saw the change come over the mayor. He approached me slowly, clenching and unclenching his hands as the rage built. A flash in his eyes sent shivers down my back and, for the first time in my life, I finally listened to my gut when it said, "Run, Jayne, run."

CHAPTER TWO

I didn't pause long enough to see if he followed me or not. I turned on my heel and bolted for the open road. Unfortunately, in my confusion, I ran to the right rather than to the left, which would have taken me closer to home or at least in the direction of other houses.

It took the mayor less than thirty seconds to start his pursuit. A stampede of wild horses slammed against my stomach, and my heart pounded at a marathon rate. I dashed from side to side, not sure which way to run. He drove like a mad bull in pursuit, lurching forward, then slowing down, laughing at me as I fled.

I didn't know where to go but, I knew this would not

end well for me if I didn't start to think more clearly. Visions of coyotes fighting over the remains of my broken body flashed in my mind. I darted to the right in a last effort to avoid the four-thousand-pound beast pursuing me. At that moment, the moon decided to play hide and seek with a cloud and I stepped off the road shoulder and tumbled down the bank. I landed hard against a prickly pear cactus.

The car skidded as he hit the brakes. After only a heartbeat, the slamming of a car door reverberated through the quiet night. In the darkness, the mayor couldn't see me, but I saw him swaying in the beam of the car's headlights.

"Come back here. I won't hurt you. I just want to talk," he purred.

I knew without a doubt he intended to lure me in, but ultimately make sure I regretted my behavior.

He called my name a few more times, "Jayne we should talk about what you think you heard. You're a sweet girl. I can be an immensely persuasive man and extremely generous to my friends. But I'm not someone you want as an enemy. I'll let you think about it while you spend the night out here. When I come back in the morning, I'm sure you will see reason." Another slow minute ticked by before he got in his car and drove off, sending a shower of loose gravel into the air.

When I finally felt safe from his wrath, I realized my

situation hadn't improved. I lay against a prickly pear cactus, with torn pants, a shoe lost during the tumble down the embankment. My hair sprung free from its clasp, I probably looked like I used an industrial size mixer as a blow dryer. I was on a little-traveled road in the dark of the night in the desert, with no way home and no cell phone. Again, I wondered how I got myself into these situations.

I winced as I sat up, definitely noticing the cactus thorns deeply imbedded in my backside. I know Prickly Pear cactus grow long spines, plus clusters of fine, tiny, barbed spines, which are difficult to see. They're even harder to remove once lodged in the skin.

I tried to climb up the slight hill, but it proved a challenging task what with the lack of street lights this far from the town. I found it even more difficult sans shoe, and with those few sips of champagne —okay, maybe it was a glass or two—snuck while serving guests. At the time, I justified drinking the champagne since it wasn't often that I had a chance to drink anything that cost a night's wages. I would remember that lesson – no alcohol on the job. No bad deed goes unpunished. Finally making it to the road, I looked around cautiously to make certain the mayor really did leave.

There I stood on the side of the road, feeling violated and disturbed. An overpowering inclination hit me to sit and let the humiliation and anguish of the night drain out of me.

Not an option, with the cactus thorns in my rear end. I needed a few minutes to wallow in self-pity. So I paused in my tousled state and let the tears roll down my cheeks. Why was I such a screw-up all the time? This was not how I expected my life to turn out but, so far, nothing had gone the way I planned. I thought making a new start in Arizona would erase my past, and I could become someone else. I would meet my cowboy and live happily ever after on my own little Ponderosa. The courage I summoned to venture across the country, I somehow left at a diner in Texas.

Wiping my nose on a piece of my torn shirt, I thought about what my Dad would say if he stood beside me at this moment. I remembered with sadness the scandal that made him leave his beloved police force only months before his retirement eligibility. I looked up to the stars, swearing his face appeared in the constellations. *I'm sorry I turned out to be such a disappointment to you, Dad.*

I took a deep breath and squared my shoulders. Time to toughen up. So, off I went, stepping cautiously with only one shoe. If I continued in the direction I headed when I left the mayor's house, this road would surely end at Bartlett Lake. The lake didn't offer any options, so I made my way back to town, which meant creeping past the mayor's. I estimated it would be at least five miles after that before I ran across any houses. Looking the way I did and at this hour, it seemed unlikely anyone would even answer the door if I knocked.

With no watch, I estimated the time since I made my escape. That would put it close to one o'clock in the morning. Luckily for me, the nights stayed warm this time of year, and sunrise would start just before six o'clock. I wasn't a fan of exercise as a lifestyle, and the farthest I usually walked was around the restaurant or a mall. That should count for something, I told myself. With no clue how I would do it, I needed to make it home. I had no choice. I was on my own.

I stumbled along in the darkness, thankful for the partial light of the moon, but eager to get nearer to town where I would feel some small sense of safety. The call of a coyote on the hunt startled me into picking up my pace. I didn't cherish the idea of becoming a late night meal for a mountain lion or pack of hungry coyotes. After practically crawling on my belly to get past the mayor's house, I made slow headway. Periodically, I stopped for a break, and indulged in a few minutes more of my pity party before carrying on.

My feet hurt—the one without the shoe more than the other. My backside stung from the prickly pear spines, and my head ached from the champagne. Most of all, though, my heart anguished over the altercation with the mayor. It occurred to me, if I just sat and waited until morning, someone might happen by. But, what if the mayor, true to his word, returned to use a not-so-pleasant method of persuasion to make me forget what I heard? Tossing that out as a plan, and because I refused to give up on anything so easily, I kept walking. Progress, even though slow, was better than nothing at all.

Another few miles and probably an hour later, I spied headlights in the distance. Relief temporarily replaced exhaustion and despite my aching body I actually skipped for a few steps. Then reality set in and I became apprehensive. What if Mayor McArthur changed his mind? Rather than waiting for morning, maybe he decided to come back and continue his disgusting attempt at flirtation. Maybe he went home for a gun so he could shoot me and leave me to die slowly, staining the desert with my blood. Maybe he sent some thugs to do to the job for him. They might spread my body parts around, cutting off my fingers so I couldn't be recognized. It could be some weird serial killer traveling the back roads looking for a lone woman in a torn wine-stained work shirt. It could be a Sheriff's Deputy on patrol or a drunk driver trying to avoid the police. I warned myself to ease up on the drama before hysteria set in. Despite my paranoia, ultimately I didn't care who was coming. Whoever it was, friend or foe, I planned to flag him or her down and hitch a ride. I was so done walking.

The lights approached at a moderate pace, bouncing over the ruts in the road. Suddenly, I worried about my appearance, in case it was a nice little old lady who would be afraid to stop for someone looking like me. I tried to fix my hair and rearrange my clothes, in the hopes I was presentable. Even for a team of hit men, I may as well look good for my last minutes alive. My mother always lectured me that first impressions were the most important. Old habits die hard.

The vehicle drew closer, and I stepped to the side of the road to make sure the driver didn't accidentally, or purposefully, run me over. I didn't want to let this opportunity pass me by—literally—so I waved my arms and jumped around as well as I could with cactus thorns in my rear end.

At the last moment, I looked around to see if I could pick up a rock or some sort of weapon, just in case I needed it. On the off chance it was the mayor, I could be prepared this time. Spying what I thought was a flat rock, I grabbed a dark object and held it behind my back.

I heard country music blasting from the stereo and the engine grinding. My heart fluttered for a second. I seriously doubted a killer would listen to George Strait at that volume.

The truck's headlights must have caught the remaining white areas on my shirt, surprising the driver into suddenly slamming on the brakes, and screeching to a halt just short of me. Neither of us moved for a moment. The driver possibly stunned to see anything looking like me on an isolated road in the middle of the night. I, considering whether I should jump back into the prickly pear or jump into the vehicle.

The driver climbed out of the truck slowly, walking around in front of the cab. He looked me up and down and shook his head. The headlights revealed a person tall and lean, dressed in worn Wrangler jeans and cowboy boots, topped off with a baseball cap.

"Did your car break down around here somewhere?" He looked around.

"Well, not exactly. I could use a ride or a phone."

"I don't have a cell phone with me, but I can give you a ride. Are you by yourself?"

For a moment I considered a lie, saying my boyfriend was behind me, but even I wouldn't have bought that one. "Yes, I'm alone," I confessed.

"Mind if I ask what you're doing out here in the middle of the night dressed like that?"

"It's kind of a long story. What brings you out this way?" I felt uncomfortable sharing the night's events, and I had experienced enough humiliation. I had no motivation to relive any part of it with a stranger.

"I like to put my boat in the water early and do a little fishing before the lake gets crowded."

"I think you may have forgotten the boat." I darted my eyes toward the back of his truck, holding tighter to my weapon.

"You're funny for a stranded young lady who looks like just she just went ten rounds with a KitchenAid. My boat is tied up at the dock. I was camping, and realized I hadn't brought my favorite fishing pole, so I drove home. I accidentally left my cell in my tent."

I looked at the truck cab more closely and saw a pair of eyes peering back at me.

"You have someone with you?"

"Yep, never travel without my favorite girl."

We both stood for another heartbeat, until he said, "Well, do you want a ride somewhere, or were you planning to hike all the way back to Carefree?"

I took a deep breath, "Yes, please. I couldn't walk another step. You can drop me any place where I can call a cab to get home." I added as an afterthought, "As long as your girlfriend doesn't mind."

"Oh, she'll mind alright. She was ready for bed three hours ago, but she'll get over it."

I cautiously moved closer to the truck, trying to get a better look at his friend, embarrassed at the sad condition of my hair and clothing. As I reached the passenger door, a loud bark greeted me, and a shaggy blond head poked out of the open window. A dog and a sense of humor, this guy was okay in my book.

"Your favorite girl?" I reached up to give her head a pat.

"That's Molly. She and I have been together for ten years. She's no pup anymore, and she hates to have her sleep schedule disturbed." He put one leg into the driver's side of the truck. "Get in. She won't bite."

"Ah, there's just one little problem," I said sheepishly.

"You don't want to ruin your good clothes riding in this old truck?"

"No, I love old trucks. It's the sitting down part I have a problem with. You see, I slipped and kind of, sort of, landed on my butt on a prickly pear."

He looked at me for a long moment, again shaking his head. Getting out of the truck, he walked around to the bed and opened a toolbox. Coming back to me, he gently took my arm and led me to the front so we stood in the glare of the headlights. Forgetting I still held the rock in my hands I tried to act inconspicuous and held it partly behind my back.

One side of his mouth twitched in a smile. "Do you realize this area is still open range?"

"You mean there are cows and horses that wander

around here, free and wild?"

"Yes. And, if you were thinking of taking that as a souvenir, you'll be riding in the back of my truck. Molly may be old, but she smells better than a cow patty." His deep laugh sent shivers up and down my spine.

Flinging my "rock" to the ground, I wished I could disappear into the darkness.

"Actually I thought it was a rock. My precaution, in case you were a serial killer." I could feel heat emanating from my every pore and reminded myself to breathe.

"You planned to beat me up with a cow patty if I turned out to be a psycho?" He chuckled. "Okay, turn around, miss, and let me see if I can pull out those spines."

I obeyed meekly. What else could go wrong this evening? Might as well have a stranger pulling cactus thorns out of my least impressive feature.

Using a pair of needle-nose pliers, he ably removed the largest of the spines sticking out of my work pants, chuckling as he worked.

"That's the best I can do at the moment. When you get home you really should use some antiseptic to make sure you don't get an infection." He gave me a little pat on the head, reminding me of the tender touch of a parent, and walked back to the driver's side door.

"Well are you coming or not?"

I wasted no more time deciding and gingerly climbed into the passenger seat, giving Molly a gentle shove to convince her to make room for me. He kept his old truck cleaner than I did my car. On the passenger side of my car, all the old soda cans rolling around amongst the candy bar wrappers barely left room for anyone's feet. But this truck looked as neat as a pin, with a pine air freshener dangling from the rear-view mirror for the extra touch.

"I'm Jonas," he said as he turned the truck around to head back in the direction he came.

"I'm Jayne. Jayne Stanford."

"Okay, Miss Jayne-Jayne Stanford. Where do you want to go?"

"Home. Right now I want to go home more than anything in the world." I meant home to Maryland with my family, but I gave him directions to my apartment.

Jonas drove the few remaining miles through Carefree and into Cave Creek. I was thankful for Molly's presence between us. I tried to peek at him from the corner of my eye without being too obvious. He looked to be about my age, or maybe a few years older, in his early thirties, well over six feet tall, slender, and possibly muscular, but I couldn't tell for sure in the dark. He liked country music, so that definitely registered as a plus, and loved animals, plus, plus.

My whole body ached with fatigue, like I'd ridden for

the entire eight seconds on a two-thousand-pound bull that stepped on me afterwards for good measure. Feeling safe for the time being, I leaned back in the seat and closed my eyes for just a minute. I must have fallen asleep, because the next thing I knew Jonas was shaking me gently.

"You're home."

I awoke with a start, forgetting for a brief second where I was. My head had tilted to the left to rest on Molly, and I was pretty sure I left some drool on her soft fur. I wanted to stay there all night with her warmth and comfort.

"Thanks for the ride. I really appreciate it. I would probably have been walking for hours," I said as I opened the door.

"No problem. It's just lucky I was heading back out to the lake. Listen, here's my card if you ever need anything, like repairs or things fixed." He handed me his business card with a bashful smile on his face.

I got out of the truck, gave Molly a last pat, and waved as he backed out and drove off. I smiled as I walked the few steps to my apartment. Maybe this night hadn't turned out so badly after all, I thought.

Opening the door of my house might have proven difficult with my purse still in the trunk of my car. Luckily for me, I routinely locked myself out and I kept a key under a potted plant. Not the best place, but it worked for me, and right now I couldn't fathom dealing with any more drama.

Once inside, my cat Bugsy gave me the usual leg bump to share his happiness at seeing me, but also verbally expressed his intense dissatisfaction at being left alone in the house for hours with his bowl empty until almost breakfast time.

I would know no peace until I fed and petted him. I did my parental duty, trying to still my shaking hands. My bed called out to me as exhaustion kicked in. I didn't recognize my reflection in the bathroom mirror... nothing short of scary. Yet, Jonas Harper gave me his business card.

Throwing my ruined work clothes and my one shoe in the pile of clothes in the corner, I flopped face down on my bed. I had to be careful not to aggravate any remaining cactus spines, and didn't even bother to pull back the covers.

Part of me was relieved I made it home in one piece after this bizarre night. Part of me wanted to spit in anger. Bugsy nuzzled my face and I pulled him close, allowing my tears to wet his silky fur.

I knew ten hours of sleep would bring me back to as close to a normal human being as I ever got. So, I tried my best to forget what had happened in the last few hours. Except, of course, for the thirty minutes at the end... that part I would leave firmly implanted in my brain.

CHAPTER THREE

I woke up to a pair of yellow eyes three inches from my face. Despite his late-night feeding, Bugsy lived by a schedule and he wouldn't let me forget breakfast time. He didn't care if the world was coming to an end, let alone that I had only slept for a few hours. He meowed in my face, giving me a nose full of morning breath.

"Okay, I'm getting up," I gently nudged him off me and rolled over to glance at the alarm clock. "It's only seven o'clock. You just ate at three thirty. You can't possibly be hungry again."

He answered me with a series of increasingly desperate meows, punctuated by a little bite to my arm.

No choice remaining but to get up. I winced as I

pulled on my favorite hanging-around-the-house shorts and t-shirt, stepped into my flip flops, and headed into the kitchen. My rear end stung from the cactus spines, and the rest of me felt like I had worked a double shift. I trudged into the kitchen, noticing the dust bunnies rolling around on the floor on my way, and prepared Bugsy's breakfast.

Popping the top on my favorite choice for caffeine, a Diet Mountain Dew, I contemplated the events of the prior night. I breathed a sigh of relief that a bad situation hadn't escalated into a life-threatening dilemma. I'm sure the mayor regretted his behavior in the light of day and would be apologetic. At least I hoped he would feel that way since I still had to go back to his house to pick up my car. I could probably hitch a ride with my friend and co-worker Emmett and, if I ran as fast as a jackrabbit, I could be in and out before the mayor even noticed my presence.

With that plan in place, I called Emmett, who acted not the least bit happy to hear from me so early on a Saturday morning.

"What?"

"Hey, it's your favorite co-worker."

"Please tell me you didn't wake me up without having a life-threatening emergency."

"Funny you should say that. Actually I need a ride. I accidentally locked my car keys in the trunk."

He let out a long exasperated breath, "If you were anyone else, I would hang up this phone and pretend you never called. I'll be over in an hour."

"I guess I'm polishing your station for the next two weeks again."

"You guessed right, Sugar."

Emmett was a stickler for promptness, so I put myself in gear. I took the quickest shower possible, which meant skipping the double conditioning treatment to tame my wild, curly locks; made sure no spines remained in my backside; and dressed in the first thing I could find clean in my pile of clothes.

My work clothes from the night before lay ruined, and I couldn't work in one shoe. This would require a visit to Goodwill before my shift tonight. I was an expert at digging through someone's castaway treasures to find suitable replacements. Normally, I love to shop, but after last night my heart wasn't in it.

While I happily munched on a toaster pastry, Emmett called to say he was outside waiting. I grabbed my spare set of keys, a second can of Dew, and ran out to meet him.

"You better not spill that crazy juice in my car." Emmett pointed at my open can of soda.

"I won't spill it."

"These seats are not faux leather. If you spill one

drop, or I find one animal hair, you'll be cleaning my car in addition to polishing my station in the restaurant." Emmett spoke like a tough guy, but I knew he was all mushy inside.

"Yeah, yeah. I hear you."

Emmett drove like he was trying to qualify at NASCAR. I didn't know who drove worse, the drunken mayor or Emmett, so I resigned myself to holding on tight and making sure not to waste a drop of soda in his car, as ordered.

When we pulled up to the mayor's house, the gate loomed up in front of us, securely closed. I figured I could climb over and slip back out again without the mayor ever noticing. At any rate, he was probably sleeping off a serious hangover. Emmett, happy to leave me behind, headed off to the gym to work on his already bulging biceps.

Fortunately, since I wanted to avoid a fatherly lecture, I hadn't told him any of what happened between the mayor and me. Since I moved to Arizona, I had constantly turned to Emmett for help. I didn't have many friends, and he had been invaluable to me in learning the restaurant business.

In the stark daylight, the cold metal gate loomed over me as a warning I wasn't welcome here. I stuffed my spare keys in my pocket, scrambled to the top of the gate. Before I could drop into the yard and, into what felt like the lion's den, the gate started opening. With one leg hanging over each side,

I hung on for dear life as I was rammed into the spiny branches of a massive Bougainvillea bush. Again? What is up with this place and the gate, I wondered to myself. Thorns pierced my skin and the branches tangled in my hair.

Hidden from view of the approaching car, I wasn't able to see who was leaving the mayor's house. I was hopeful it might be the mayor, and so would avoid any possibility of a re-run of last night.

After the gate closed and the sound of the car became distant, I climbed down. The driveway stretched endlessly, and the estate rose before me threatening, yet beckoning. The sound of my shoes crunching on the gravel and the muffled jangling of my keys echoed in my ears. The hairs on the back of my neck stood up, and I chewed on the nub of a fingernail while I hurried toward the house. I glanced over my shoulder and gave an involuntary shudder. This place looked creepier in the daylight than it did last night.

My car sat like a lone sentry in the driveway, so I assumed the car which opened the gate was either Tami Lynn departing in her "walk of shame" or, as I hoped, the mayor leaving. In my mad sprint to freedom last night, I didn't remember seeing her car - or much of anything... besides the closed gate.

Releasing the breath I didn't realize I held, I reached my car and used my spare keys to open the trunk. My purse rested beneath the box of empty wine bottles. I dug it out. As I started to leave, I remembered leaving my apron on the stool in the kitchen. It was the only decent one I owned, and all of my tips from the night before remained in the pocket. I definitely couldn't leave the tips behind. Just my luck, I would need to knock on the door, or try to inconspicuously sneak in the back to grab my apron.

I opted for Plan B. No point in disturbing the mayor, if he was at home, when I could be in and out in a flash. I tiptoed around to the back, praying the door to the kitchen wasn't locked. Hey, the house was gated and really far from town, right? Hopefully the mayor had not already observed my approach and decided to wait for me to begin round two.

Before exposing myself fully, I decided to take a quick peek inside the house. If the mayor was up and about, I might have to switch back to Plan A.

Picturing the layout in my mind, I opted for a window I believed would look into the eat-in kitchen area, but still keep me from being fully exposed to anyone on the inside. I crawled under the poisonous leafy branches of an oleander bush to get closer, hoping I didn't have a close encounter with a tarantula or black widow. I feared bugs that could fly and nest in my hair more than spiders, but I had no desire to be bitten. I could reach the bottom of the window with my fingertips, but couldn't see in. So, I set one foot on a small box, which looked like it might control the sprinkler system. With a grunt and a hop, I managed to get myself high enough to see in.

The kitchen looked clear but, unexpectedly, I heard uneven footsteps treading on the gravel behind me. I dropped down from the ledge and squished myself behind the oleander, hoping no one saw me.

If I simply chose to walk up to the front door and knock, I could have had my apron back and been on my way. Why not do something the easy way for a change, instead of always taking the harder path? Instead, I now looked like a stalker peering in the mayor's windows. I held my breath and froze, listening for any indication that I had been seen. The person paused momentarily, but continued by with a sort of clomping sound, and entered the house.

Grabbing my opportunity, I darted from the shrubbery back to my car. Feeling unsettled and oddly guilty for my voyeuristic episode, I hopped in and started the ignition, hoping for a rapid escape from the property. If I was lucky, no one would hear my clunky 1990 Honda Accord, as we rattled to the gate. I tapped my fingers on the steering wheel, impatient for the gate to open wide enough to slip through. Why is it, the more I try to hurry, the slower the rest of the world seems to move? I didn't get my tips, but at least I retrieved my car. Maybe I could try again later in the day when I had gathered my wits and a bit more courage.

Next stop... try to find a decent used pair of work shoes and another shirt. Fingers crossed I could pick up both at the Goodwill store for under five dollars, the amount in my wallet. I hoped for a busy night at the restaurant tonight so I could make up for the loss of last night's wages.

Maybe the act of shopping would settle my raw nerves and the bad taste that filled my mouth whenever I came anywhere near the mayor.

A few hours and several Goodwill credit card charges later, I stopped off at my best friend Bailey's mini-ranch to take care of the chores. Bailey brought animals home on a regular basis, and those she didn't pick up somehow found her. It created a never-ending cycle, to care for so many rescue animals, but I appreciated Bailey for taking them all in. Whenever she was out of town on business, I filled in full time in "loco parentis," as she would say. It sounded to me like "crazy parent," which pretty accurately described the responsibilities.

I chuckled at the thought of petite Bailey, in her flowing hippie-style skirts and stack of bracelets clanging, struggling with a wheelbarrow full of manure. At the same time, she would rattle off technical mumbo jumbo into her headset with someone in a foreign country. She tried more than once to describe to me what she did for a living. All I could ever remember was it had something to do with keeping a company's information secure from outside attacks by someone or something. She could chatter on for hours about application security breaches, firewalls, cyber-attacks and electronic monitoring. Sadly, after the first ten minutes, my brain started to hurt. Whatever it was she did, it paid her a nice enough salary, and allowed her to support all of her four-legged children. Somehow she managed to find new families for many and kept only those no one would adopt.

First, to the pens to feed Jasper the blind horse and Billy the three-legged goat, and throw some feed out for my least favorite, Danny the rooster. That wicked bird escaped from the safety of his pen last week, causing me to be late for work. After forty minutes, I was ready to let him take his chances with the coyotes, or maybe fry him up myself for dinner. My inability to look Bailey in the eye and try to explain what happened to him saved his life. Okay, so maybe I couldn't actually see myself cooking him, but I was mad enough at the time to threaten it.

Dogs and cats ran circles around my legs, anxious for attention as much as food. After that, I mucked out the pens and put out fresh water for the rabbits, round-tailed ground squirrels, and cactus wrens. Occasionally, I provided sustenance for the wild Javelina or burros that wandered by. Lastly, I went inside her cozy little adobe ranch house and cared for the indoor zoo.

A few hours later the chores done, I showered, dressed in my new semi-used clothes and— best of all—on time for a change, I strolled in the back entrance to the restaurant. Heat from the ovens slapped me in the face as head chef, Sal shouted orders to the line cooks. The scent of rosemary chicken blended with freshly baked carrot cake. Knives whirred over cutting boards chopping vegetables for sides and salads.

I waved as I made my way to the dining room, known as the front of the house. A glance at the reservations showed few bookings, it looked like another slow night ahead. Standing at the end of the bar, I watched the clock tick minute by minute, hoping I could make enough in tips to keep the electricity on for another month.

Just as I was about to beg to be sent home early, a familiar-looking man entered the restaurant and took a seat at the end of the bar. My heart did a little flutter, and I swore all of the nerves in my body tingled. My rescuer... or, as I liked to think of him, man with cute dog in pickup truck. Despite myself, I had thought about him all day. Looking different than last night, Jonas wore a black-felt cowboy hat and a well-starched western shirt. Those blue eyes could mesmerize the clothes off any girl.

Emmett strolled up beside me with a wicked grin. His

extreme white teeth almost glowed against the darkness of his spray-on tan. "Check out the hottie at the end of the bar. Is he a fine specimen of a man or what?"

"Stop staring. Oh no, he's looking this way." I did the first thing that crossed my mind and ran into the kitchen to hide.

Emmett followed me, laughing. "What just happened?"

"He's the one who picked me up last night in the desert after the incident with the mayor."

"What?"

Remembering I hadn't told Emmett about the mayor's molestation, I gave him a watered down version of what happened.

After a rant on what should happen to jerks who take advantage of naïve girls, and a strongly worded lecture on the importance self-defense, he said, "So why are you hiding from that guy at the bar? Did you happen to forget to tell me he spent the night with you?"

"Really, Emmett, you know I'm not like that and, besides, look at him. He's gorgeous and I'm, well you know." I looked down at myself temporarily clean and tidy.

"Girl, you need to go out there and put your flirt on." Emmett dug in his apron pocket and produced a travel size tube of hair gel, "Stand still and let me fix your hair."

I swatted his hand away, "What should I say?"

"How about thanks for taking me home, and would you like to come over later to have me for dessert? How about a touch of lip gloss?

"You're a bad boy."

"If you decide you don't want him, let me know because I'm sure I could convince him to switch sides."

Laughing, Emmett grabbed my hand and dragged me out of the kitchen, and I saw Jonas looking over a menu. Mercifully, this allowed me to avoid eye contact with him until I could form a proper sentence. As luck would have it, I didn't get another chance to catch my breath for an hour. Each time I ran back and forth between the kitchen and the dining room, I furtively glanced over to see if Jonas was still there.

Fifteen happy diners later, I gathered my courage and marched to the end of the bar as Jonas sipped a cup of coffee.

"Hi."

Jonas smiled, and I stopped breathing, "Hi Jayne-Jayne Stanford."

"I wanted to thank you again for helping me out last night. I'd probably still be walking if you hadn't come along when you did."

"I'm sure, by now, you would have made it back to

civilization."

"What brings you to Wild Bronco?"

Jonas looked around, "It's a restaurant. I like to eat."

Duh, Jayne, what a stupid thing to say. "I mean it's a coincidence that you're here where I work, and I've never seen you before."

"Actually, you had your name tag on last night, and I was curious."

A flash of inspiration hit. "I'm having a few friends over for dinner tomorrow. If you're free maybe you would like to join us, and I could repay you with a home-cooked meal."

Jonas cocked his head to one side, apparently considering the offer. "That sounds really nice. What time?"

"How about six-thirty?"

"I'll be there. Maybe you should give me your phone number in case I get lost." He smiled that same bashful smile, which lit up his eyes and turned me into a puddle.

I wrote my number down on a cocktail napkin and he tucked it in his shirt pocket.

I noticed my last table looking around for me. "I better get back to work before my boss catches me. I'll see you tomorrow night."

I hurried to my table before Jonas witnessed my heart beating through my shirt. Emmett must have rubbed off on me... I'd never asked a man on a date before. Officially, this wasn't a date, even though Jonas didn't know I hadn't made any dinner plans with friends. Now, I needed to scurry around and recruit some people to come over.

My mind raced with all of the preparations. First, figure out a menu I could make on a limited budget. Clean the apartment, find some recipes, clean the apartment, find something to wear, clean the apartment. Okay, first on the list... clean the apartment.

In the kitchen, I was feverishly polishing my glassware when my manager Peter sought me out.

"There's someone up front to see you."

Hoping for Jonas, I skipped out happily thinking he wanted to say good-bye before he left. But Jonas already left the bar. Instead, I slid to a stop as a complete stranger turned toward me. He stood ramrod stiff, and wore a shiny badge clipped to his belt.

"Ms. Stanford?"

"Yes, that's me. Can I help you?" I racked my brain to try to remember if I cruised through photo radar recently.

"I'm Detective Tim Stewart. I would like to ask you a few questions about your relationship to mayor Franklin McArthur."

"Relationship?"

"What were you doing last night at the mayor's

house?"

"I worked a party there."

"Perhaps we could talk more privately?" The detective looked over my shoulder.

Following his gaze, I could see not only Peter the manager hovering nearby, but pretty much the entire restaurant paused to focus on my drama.

"We could go out front for a minute, but my shift isn't over yet."

He abruptly turned and marched out the front door with me trailing reluctantly on his heels. Questions swirled around my brain, every one of which I was afraid to ask.

"Ms. Stanford, when you left the mayor's house this morning what condition would you say the mayor was in?"

"I didn't see him this morning. I went back to pick up my car, but no one was around. I didn't knock on the door because I didn't want to wake him."

"Is that your story?"

"Yes. I mean, that's the truth. Emmett dropped me off, I got my car and left."

"You are saying you didn't spend the night with the mayor last night? Interesting that I have a witness who saw you in the house last night after the guests left. You were alone with the mayor, and argued. Do you deny that?" He leaned closer to me. "Wasn't your vehicle parked at his house all night? Didn't you leave in a hurry this morning before the police could be called?"

"Yes, I mean, no. I didn't spend the night with the mayor. I got a ride home because I locked my keys in my car, and I went back this morning to pick it up. What is this about?" I heard a little voice screaming at me to shut up.

"The housekeeper found the mayor dead earlier today, and it seems you were the last person to see him alive."

"No way! I mean, that's terrible."

"The evidence indicates a struggle in the kitchen, and I'm willing to bet my next paycheck that the scratch on his cheek came from a woman, namely you."

"The mayor came on to me and we scuffled, but he was fine the last time I saw him. Did he have an accident?"

"If you mean did he accidentally fall on a knife and stab himself multiple times, then I suppose you could call that an accident. In my profession we call that homicide."

CHAPTER FOUR

It took me the next hour, while feverishly polishing wine glasses, to absorb the shock of what the detective said to me. He advised me not to leave town and added that I could expect to hear from him again *soon*. Although he didn't exactly say the words, it looked like he just posted me as the nightly special on the menu for murder.

I wondered what witness claimed to overhear my "argument" with the mayor. Did that person understand the difference between a lovers' quarrel and a woman fighting off unwanted advances? Was it Tami Lynn, in a semi-conscious state, who thought she heard something else? I needed to find her and make sure she didn't misunderstand. If the housekeeper found his body, who drove out of the estate as I sat perched on the gate?

As we walked out to our cars to leave, I leaned on Emmett's strong shoulder for support.

"What should I do?"

Emmett elbowed me. "Didn't you tell me last week the next time he came in and tried to grope you that he would get what was coming to him?"

"This isn't a joke. You know I didn't kill him."

"You won't even kill a fly in the kitchen. Of course I know you didn't do it. I was the one you dragged out of bed early this morning to fetch your car. Stop worrying, this will all be fine tomorrow."

"I hope you're right. Even if I wasn't his biggest fan, it gives me chills to think maybe I was one of the last people to see him alive." I tried to give Emmett a hug.

He held me at arm's length instead. "Oh, no you don't, sloppy Sally. Do you see how clean my shirt is and how not clean yours is?"

"Hey, I didn't drop or spill anything on a guest all night long. It's a new record."

"Not on anyone *else*. Looks like you sacrificed yourself for a change."

His words rang true. My shirt made a poor imitation of Jackson Pollock art. Splotches of food and wine covered the front. I even managed to have something that looked like a gravy stain running down my back. I shrugged my shoulders and headed across the parking lot to the far space where I parked Betsy.

I only made it a few steps before I remembered my plans with Jonas. I turned back. "Emmett, I almost forgot to ask you to come by tomorrow night for dinner. I've invited Jonas over as a thank you, but told him I was having a few friends. Can you come and bring a date?"

"Sorry, babe, but I have other plans for tomorrow."

"I need you there! What am I going to say if no one else shows up? He'll know I lied."

"You can't wait until the last minute to invite me to a party. I'm a popular guy. Besides, you'll have a lot more fun if it's just you two."

"Geez, thanks for nothing," I mumbled.

He hopped in his car and roared out of the parking lot.

Before I reached my car, the hostess Ashley called to me from the restaurant.

"I almost forgot to tell you that someone left you a note at the hostess stand."

Curious, I trudged back and took the folded piece of plain white paper from her hand.

Meet me at the Rodeo Grounds when you get off work. I have information for you about the mayor.

The rodeo grounds weren't on my way home, but the

detour would take me only fifteen minutes outside of Cave Creek. I figured I could stop off, and be home within a half hour. I couldn't imagine who would want to meet me, especially this late in the evening, or what information that person could possibly want to give me. Why not call the police and tell them whatever he or she knew about the mayor? Silly question coming from me. I developed a solid distrust of the police after they wrongly accused my father of taking bribes while he was on the force. If he hadn't been pressured to resign from the police department, he might not have gone out on the boat with me that fateful day.

Whatever the reason for someone leaving me a note, I felt jittery. I took these same steps five nights a week but adding this note to the events of the last two days made me feel uneasy. Chewing on my stubby fingernail, I kept glancing over my shoulder to make sure no one followed me. I fidgeted with my purse and dug out my keys. When I finally reached Betsy, I released the breath I held, and unlocked her doors. One too many scary movies made me peek into the back seat just to be sure it remained empty.

The light breeze coming in my partially open window carried the scents of spring blooms. If I paid attention, I could sniff out the sweet perfume of the orange blossoms from someone's back yard, the light scent of the purple sage, and the night-blooming cactus. I loved this time of year in

Arizona because it wasn't yet hot during the day, and the nights stayed chilly enough to sit by a fire pit gazing at the stars. The town of Cave Creek sat far enough north of the city of Phoenix, and the lack of streetlights on all but the primary roads made the sky glitter like sequins on a rodeo queen's western shirt.

I drove out of town and turned right onto Carefree Highway. The highway, devoid of cars, stretched like a black ribbon, inviting a few coyotes that trotted along the shoulder to hunt for dinner. I spontaneously tightened my grip on the wheel, concerned for their safety as much as my own, in case one of them dashed across the road at the last minute.

Turning onto 32nd Street, I found the entrance to the rodeo grounds and drove around looking for another car. The grounds seemed forlorn without the reverberating sound of cheering crowds and the stamping of two-toed hooves. Developing my love of the rodeo as a young girl, I grabbed every opportunity to sit in the hard wooden stands. Bordered by the majestic Sonoran mountains, I imagined the area remained much like it had for the first English settlers. Odd that in fifteen miles, I could be in downtown Phoenix enclosed in a crust of car pollution and swallowed whole by the masses. North of the city, Cave Creek and her sister town Carefree, still cling tightly to their old west history. Exactly why so many people flock here from October to May, and why I selected it as the place to have a new life.

Without the moon to light the arena, only the path of my headlights sweeping over the dirt illuminated the absolute darkness. I drove, bordered on each side by metal bars defining the pens, to the opposite side of the arena. There in the corrals, rodeo hands unload and hold bulls and broncs to await their eight seconds in the spotlight. Not finding another car in the contestant area, I drove back to the main lot and backed up beside the Cowboy Kitchen food shack, which looked like it had seen better days.

I rolled my window all the way down to enjoy a moment of peace after my crazy night. I inhaled the aromas lingering around the grounds. If I sat completely still, I imagined I could hear the loud call of the announcer getting the crowd excited for the next ride, and the snorting and stomping of the bulls in anticipation. I could feel their hot breath on my skin, and smell the sweat from the cowboys as they ambled out of the arena after a rough ride, shaking the dust from their hats.

I took the time to ponder the events of the last two days. Who really murdered the mayor and why? Could it have been Trent Hayworth or someone else with a vendetta? Was it the housekeeper I heard as I cowered in the bushes, or was it the killer?

A dog howled frantically somewhere close by,

interrupting the solitude of the moment. The beam of my headlights captured the yellow glint of a mountain lion and I felt his low growl roll over my skin. Glancing anxiously in my rear-view mirror, I kept an eye behind me in case someone strolled out from the food shack. I rolled up my window and double-checked that both doors were locked, in case one of the abandoned bales of straw took on a life of its own and moved closer. I jumped in my seat as a metal gate clanked open and shut in the breezy night air.

After fifteen minutes, I wiped my now sweaty palms on my pants and gave up on the idea of anyone actually showing up. I started the car to leave, just as another vehicle was pulling into the lot. It's about darn time, I thought.

I watched as a dark older model sedan drove slowly past me, circled once and then drove off to the other side of the parking area. The car backed up and turned off its lights. I waited to see if someone would approach me. When no one did I decided I would have to walk over to see what information he or she had and if it was worth all this drama.

Before I could even unhook my seatbelt, a police cruiser rolled into the lot. He shined his lights on me and then drove over to the other car. Uh oh, this is getting more interesting by the minute, I thought.

An officer exited the cruiser and spoke a few words to the occupant of the car and then headed to me.

He pulled up in front of my car, blocking my exit and parked. He approached me with his hand on his gun belt and one on his baton.

I rolled down my window. "Good evening officer."

"Miss, can you explain what you are doing here?"

"I was waiting for someone."

"A bit late for that wouldn't you say?

"Not if you're a server." I don't know what made me to decide to be flippant with my response when he still had his hand on his gun.

"Time to move on. We've had reports of drug dealings around here and I wouldn't want to think you were involved."

"Absolutely not. I really was waiting for someone but I guess he or she isn't showing up."

"You don't know who you're meeting?"

Geez, that did sound stupid when he said it like that. I started my car, "I'm heading home right now."

"Good idea. Make sure you don't come back."

"By the way, who was in the other car? Maybe that's who I was supposed to meet."

"I doubt it unless you were planning to hook up with two teenagers who wanted a make-out session. Is that why you're here?"

"No! Do I look like I'm cruising for teenagers?"

"I've seen all kinds."

"I'm leaving and trust me I won't be back here."

The sedan with teenagers in lust and the police officer turned right and I turned left, muttering some four-letter words that would warrant dollars in my cuss jar as I left. If this was someone's idea of a joke, it wasn't funny. In fact, it was pretty freaky.

In a moment of inspiration, I had the brilliant idea to cut across Leaping Lizard Road to save me a couple of miles. The road wasn't used much, and sported gravel all the way into town, but it was an unlikely route for drunk drivers, plus it would save me the time of going all the way back to the main road.

I rolled along contentedly, singing at the top of my lungs to Marty Robbins on the car's cassette player in an effort to calm my nerves. A pair of headlights on high beam swiftly approached, blinding me. I assumed someone on his or her way home decided to take the same shortcut as me. Wrong. The lights came close enough to kiss Betsy's bumper.

Clutching the steering wheel, I sped up, trying to prevent a spinout around a curve. Betsy's engine groaned as I spurred her to move faster, and put two wheels on the right shoulder. Despite my efforts, an ominous black Hummer with a cow-catcher on the front grill, pulled up beside me.

Darting a quick glance, I could not see the driver

through the heavily tinted windows. Thinking they wanted to pass, I let up off the gas. With the next breath, the Hummer slammed into my driver's side door, catching me off-guard, and shooting my car over the right side of the road. I scrambled to take control, but my old headstrong sedan was determined to continue her course into the rough terrain. Betsy, acting like a young filly, seemed to gain speed as we shot through the devil's claw, fairy duster, and brittlebush, heading straight for a giant Saguaro. The Hummer's lights danced behind, tracking me closely through the prickly desert underbrush.

I barely escaped ramming into the two-ton Saguaro, but not the thorny Ocotillo cactus reaching out with spindly arms to grab at the tires and claw at Betsy's sides. Loose change, old soda cans, and the entire contents of my purse flew around the inside of the car in a mini tornado, while I clenched the steering wheel to try to maintain control. I swerved around a Palo Verde tree, just missing it by inches, and tried to turn back toward the road. The Hummer cut me off and again raced beside me. Panicked and hysterically struggling to escape this crazy person, I wrenched the steering wheel in the opposite direction, sending a sharp stabbing pain through my neck and shoulder.

Like a carnival fun house, cacti, Palo Verde, and boulders jumped in front of me. Captured in my glaring headlights at the last second, they barely left time for me to swerve. Whichever way I turned, the Hummer remained right beside me, almost herding me in a purposeful direction. Betsy's transmission ground, and I heard someone screaming in terror. It was me.

My windshield clouded with desert dust. In my incoherent state, I must have turned back into my own path. Heart thudding, I suddenly related to the bucking bull, giving his heart and soul into throwing the cowboy. Even when he accomplishes the feat, he isn't free—another one always waits in the wings to climb on his back. I lost all sense of direction and didn't know which way was up. Desperate to escape, but only becoming more confused and alarmed, I was unable to shake the Hummer or find my way back to the road.

The Hummer decelerated abruptly and changed course. For a split second, I thought the ordeal was over, and my pursuer had gotten bored with the game. In only another second, my headlights discovered the reason for the Hummer's change in direction. Immediately in front of me, the arid desert soil disintegrated into a shallow ravine. Even my heightened reactions didn't prevent my car from doing a handstand in the soft sand at the bottom, leaving the back tires precariously on the edge of the bank. Despite my seat belt, the crash flung me forward like a rocket, slamming my chest against the rigid steering wheel. Betsy's pre-airbag body knocked the wind out of me in a whoosh.

I choked on a cyclone of sand. It poured in my shattered driver's side window like waves crashing over a capsized boat. Warm liquid streamed into my eye and down my left cheek. Wildly, I clawed at the seat belt trying to free myself from its grasp, while Betsy teetered, trying to decide if she should flip over the rest of the way onto the roof or maintain the ninety-degree angle. I was drowning, but without the water. Memories of a childhood tragedy flooded my brain.

I sensed, more than saw, the Hummer returning. Surely the prankster now regretted his action, and arrived to help me.

"Help! Help me please," I wailed.

Once again, I misjudged my attacker's intentions. I felt the Hummer slam into the trunk, using the cow-catcher to give Betsy the final push into the bottom of the wash. The car somersaulted onto the roof, and back upright again from the impact. The sound of laughing rang in my ears, and my world went dark.

Hours must have passed, because when I next tried to open my eyes, the scorching rays of the sun sizzled my skin. I rubbed crusted matter from my eyes. My body felt as if a team of Clydesdales dragged it behind their wagon. My head throbbed, and my right arm tingled from having lain on it for hours.

The terror of the previous night battered me with full force. Shattered bits of glass covered me, and a dried substance—I suspected blood—matted my hair on the left side. Cautiously, I unhooked the seat belt, and speculated as to whether the mysterious Hummer driver lurked nearby. The driver's side door stuck, so I crawled across the seat and forced open the passenger door, listening for any sound over the throbbing of my own heart. Fear churned my stomach, and bile rose in my throat. Gingerly crawling out of the car, my senses went on maximum alert as I surveyed the area.

I found myself utterly and completely alone.

Betsy was sunken into the deep sand at the bottom of the wash, with brush tangled in her undercarriage, scratches running all along the passenger side, and significant dents in the driver's side and the roof. As much as I could tell from my limited car knowledge, the engine hadn't fallen out despite our wild ride. I tentatively wriggled back in to determine the odds of me driving out of the wash. The keys dangled in the ignition, but nothing happened when I tried to start her. Dead battery. Better than dead Jayne, I thought to myself.

I shook my head gently to clear the fog from my brain and to think clearly about what to do. I considered the option of walking, but wasn't sure which direction and how far I would need to go before I found help. Discarding that thought as quickly as it had cropped up, I acknowledged I was in no condition to wander around the desert.

A humming sound came from someplace on the floor of my car. My initial reaction was to jump out and run, in case a snake or some feral beast crept in for shelter in the night. But the humming persisted and I realized it was my cell phone. I followed the sound, crawling on the floor and reaching my hand hesitantly under the seats. I pulled out an empty Mountain Dew can, an old half-eaten candy bar (which caused my empty stomach to protest), some loose change, a hairbrush which must have fallen out of my purse, and finally my phone.

Flipping open the old thing, I saw five missed calls. I was more popular than I thought. Actually, the numbers belonged to Bailey, Emmett, and one I didn't recognize. How lucky to have two people in my life I could count on—well, that, and a cell phone with a pretty good battery life.

Before I could press speed dial for Emmett, the phone vibrated in my hand.

Thinking it was Emmett calling again, I answered with my usual cry for help, "I am so glad you called. I really need you right now."

A pause on the other end turned into Jonas' voice. "Dinner is sounding better and better."

Despite my circumstances I still managed to feel the

embarrassment, "I thought you were my friend Emmett calling."

"Will I do?"

I couldn't help myself, I started to cry into the phone. Not the nice, light, tear-trickling-down-my-cheek, damsel-in-distress kind of cry; but the hard, gut wrenching, hysterical sobbing you do when you've reached the point of crazy. Between my sobs, I managed to tell Jonas an abbreviated version of what happened, ending with a general, "I don't know what to do."

"Are you hurt?" He didn't permit me to answer. "I ride my horse in that area so I know it well. I'm on my way. Stay right where you are, and keep the phone handy. I'll be there in ten minutes." He disconnected with a click.

"I think I'm okay. I hit my head and I'm sore, but nothing's broken." I said more to reassure myself, since no one else was listening.

No doubt, I would stay where I was... unless a black Hummer suddenly appeared to finish the job. I wondered how Jonas planned to find me when I didn't even know myself where I was. I figured it might be best to try to make it up the bank to see if I could get my bearings.

I half crawled, half stumbled, grabbing onto brittlebush to pull myself up the bank. Thankfully, without a cloud in the sky, I didn't need to worry about a sudden rainstorm pouring water down the wash in a flash flood. I shuddered at the thought, again remembering the feelings last night had dredged up. I couldn't relive those long suppressed nightmares from my childhood, not if I wanted to keep some semblance of sanity.

I reached the top and surveyed the area. In the distance, I distinguished a few houses, and even a lone car kicking up dust as it drove along the road. I concluded it must be Lazy Lizard Drive, and wondered how Jonas would ever see me this far from the road. I could see the path of destruction left in my wake when careening through the desert last night. I considered the merits of walking toward the road to meet Jonas, took a few tentative steps, and decided against it. Each step made my head explode and dizziness roll over me. I sat down abruptly, taking deep gulps of air, and placed my head between my knees to try to keep from passing out again. Jonas would just have to find me as best he could.

My phone vibrated again.

"Jayne, I've been calling you for hours. Where have you been?" Bailey demanded.

"You won't believe my last twenty-four hours. I broke a glass before the shift even started, ran around like a crazy woman for four hours, haven't had any chocolate, the mayor was murdered, and some lunatic in a Hummer ran me off the road," I said without taking a breath.

"Slow down. You're not making any sense. All I got was something about chocolate, murder, and a Hummer. Start from the beginning. And where are you now?"

"I'm still out in the desert someplace, but Jonas is on his way." I stood up.

"Jonas?"

"I have so much to tell you, but I'll have to fill you in later. My head hurts and I think I can see Jonas's truck going down the road. He should be here in a minute. I'll call you when I get back to my apartment." I hung up before I told Bailey about the murder.

I watched Jonas barreling down Lazy Lizard and come to an abrupt stop, which sent a cloud of dust spiraling around his truck. He backed up a few yards, and turned into the desert toward me. Even from this distance, I saw Molly, with her head hanging out the passenger window, ears blowing straight out behind her and tongue flopping merrily. Maybe it was just the bump on my head, or maybe the joy expressed in Molly's face, but something about this guy and the way he kept rescuing me. It touched feelings I had been trying hard to suppress for a long time.

When Jonas pulled up beside me, I was still standing there, lost in emotions that threatened to overwhelm me. Molly leapt out, almost knocking me off my feet in her exuberance. Jonas followed close on her heels, but he held me at arm's length while he looked me up and down with a grimace on his face.

"You look like you've been on a long hard ride." Jonas's words sounded harsh, but his touch felt gentle as he cupped my face in his hands. "Darlin', I think we need to get you to the hospital. You're not looking good right now."

"I don't want to go to the hospital. They'll charge me hundreds of dollars to wash my face and send me on my way. I can't afford it. Can't you just take me home?" I wiped my runny nose on the back of my hand in true girly fashion.

"Okay, one step at a time. Let's get you in the truck, and I'll take a quick look at the damage to your car. See if I can get it out of the wash without too much trouble. There's a bottle of water in the console. Have a drink and rest for a minute."

I did as I was told, and sank into the cushiony comfort of his truck. Molly busily sniffed around while Jonas climbed down into the wash to assess the damage. Taking a sip of the water eased the dryness in my throat, and I ventured a glance in the vanity mirror to evaluate my own damages. I looked as bad as I felt. My left eye puffed angrily and threatened to turn a lovely shade of purple. A cut above the eye explained my recollection of something warm running down my face. Dirt and dried blood caked my hair. My teeth felt like they'd chewed on a wool sweater, and my clothes proved irreversibly rumpled and stained.

I saw Jonas and Molly crawl up out of the wash. He shook his head and talked to the dog, or himself, I wasn't sure which.

He leaned on the driver's side window frame. "It's pretty messed up, but it may run. I'll need to get down in there and jump-start the battery. Probably can pump up the tires enough to drive to see if it can be repaired. The driver's side door is banged up, but I should be able to pry it open. I'm not sure about the roof, but that won't affect the driving as long as you don't hit your head on it. All in all, I think you were really lucky." He climbed in the truck. "Try to tell me what happened, but this time go slowly and breathe," he instructed.

"A crazy person in a huge Hummer chased me through the desert." Tears welled up in my eyes as I relived my fear.

"We should call the police," Jonas suggested.

"I can't talk about this anymore right now. I just want to go home, hug my kitty, and soak in a warm bath for three hours." I leaned against Molly for comfort. With that, Jonas took me home, and I attempted to wash away the memories haunting me, which had little to do with the events of last night, and more with the drowning death of my father.

CHAPTER FIVE

Safely home and ensconced in my tub, with half a bottle of bubbles thrown in for good measure, I sipped a cup of hot tea and went over the details of what happened. Bugsy sat on the edge of the tub dropping his string toy into the water and waiting for me to retrieve it in a never-ending cycle. Obviously, he wasn't too concerned about my ordeal once I fed and petted him. I loved that about Bugsy. He never judged me, no matter how much I screwed up my life.

"We need to call the Sheriff's Department and report this," Jonas called to me from the living room where he and Molly had settled in.

"I don't know what I would tell them. I couldn't see the person's face, and didn't get a license plate number. Not that I would have thought of it in those circumstances. I was more worried about not crashing," I said miserably.

"Finish up in there and come have some breakfast. I'll run back out to your car, and see if my friend Ray and I can get it out of the wash and running again."

The depth of my hunger surprised me. I polished off three scrambled eggs, bacon, toast, and two glasses of juice. Even more surprising, not only did Jonas manage to find that food in my apartment, he also cooked it.

Satisfied and clean, with my cut determined to be minor, and aspirin kicking in for the headache, I must have dozed off.

Hours later, I sat up slowly, still feeling the effects of the accident, but figured I would survive without needing the emergency room. Bugsy lay beside me in his usual place and snored softly. His contentment had a way of rubbing off on me. Wandering into the kitchen, I found a note on the counter from Jonas. He had spoken to his friend and they planned to tow my car to Ray's shop. Based on the description Jonas gave, Ray's preliminary guess was I wouldn't be driving it for at least the next few days.

In the meantime, I owed Bailey an update. My phone had vibrated a dozen more times, but I was too happy in dreamland to wake up enough to answer it.

"I've been so worried about you. What the heck is going on?" Bailey demanded as soon as she answered the phone.

I filled her in on all of the particulars of my last few days, beginning with the time I agreed to work the cocktail party and ending with Jonas making me breakfast.

"What am I going to do with you? I suppose a better question is, what would I ever do if something bad happened to you?"

"Don't worry, I'm resilient." I hated for Bailey to worry about me when she already had enough on her plate with work and the mini zoo. "I suppose I'll have to report this to my insurance and get a rental so I can get to work. I really can't afford to miss any nights at Wild Bronco," I said and with a slight catch in my voice. "That old car isn't worth much, but she runs well and it's all I've got."

"You can use the Mercedes," she offered.

"That is really nice, but do you remember what the inside of my car usually looks like? Besides, you know I'm slightly accident-prone. If something happened to your car, I would never forgive myself."

"It's collecting dust in my garage. I can't drive it so you may as well use it."

I thanked her again, but decided it was better for our friendship for me to rent a car than to use hers. Bailey didn't drive. Not that she couldn't drive, but getting behind the wheel terrified her. In our brief friendship, she had sidestepped any discussion about why she wouldn't drive or when she stopped doing it. Since I had known her, she always hired a car to take her to the airport and run errands, or I did it for her. She was a true friend to me and I knew whatever I needed she would be there in a heartbeat, even if she had to walk. When she was ready to tell me the story, I knew she would.

I promised I would pick up any supplies she needed for the animals after I got the rental. I pulled on some clothes and gently applied enough make-up to cover the bruising on my face, and pulled my bangs down over the cut.

I called Emmett to help me out once again. He mumbled curses the entire time, but drove me over to pick up the only car my insurance would cover. It was a tiny subcompact, which made me feel like I could put it in my pocket instead of parking it on the street. It did have power windows, a great stereo, and a navigation system.

Laughing to myself, I wondered why I would ever need a GPS to get around the small town of Cave Creek. Even with my somewhat challenged general sense of direction, the town didn't provide many streets to navigate. Besides, the only places I ever went included work, One Eyed Jack's Saloon, and the grocery store. Those, I could find easily the first few days I lived here.

I headed home to get ready for work because, despite

the stiffness in my body and soreness in my chest from hitting the steering wheel, I had picked up an extra shift. No work equals no pay for a server, and now I would have to pay for car repairs. I had postponed my dinner with Jonas, and he didn't seem to mind. Either he sympathized with the situation, or maybe was tired of rescuing me already.

I pulled the rental car into the reserved parking spot in front of my first-floor apartment. Stopping at the communal mailbox, I grabbed my mail and started up the walk. I could see Bugsy sitting in the window, peaking around the curtains, his face partially hidden by the overgrown oleander bushes outside my window. He didn't recognize the sound of the rental car, so he either sat there watching for birds or waiting for me to return. His pink nose twitched and his mouth opened in a meowed greeting when he saw me nearing. My heart did a little flip flop. I loved that old cat, and he had been through good times and bad with me. I knew he was getting on in years but couldn't imagine not having him to greet me at the door whenever I came home. I guess this is what you get when you haven't had children yet—you become the crazy cat lady. Men would come and go but, at least with a cat, I knew what to expect.

I tossed the mail on the kitchen counter and, carrying Bugsy with me, went in to assess the work uniform situation. With last night's clothes still a mess, I would need to iron a fresh shirt and clean my shoes. I didn't want to be late for the pre-shift meeting, and I hadn't eaten since the breakfast Jonas prepared, so I needed to hurry.

I buzzed to work in my little rental, and made it in time to sample the nightly specials: a melt-in-your-mouth filet with peppercorn sauce, halibut with a prosciutto and caper white wine sauce, and a trio of profiteroles for dessert.

Peter offered a bottle of wine to anyone who sold the most specials. I loved a challenge, and made up my mind to sell the most. I would prepare a lovely dinner and serve the wine to Jonas to show him how much I appreciated all he did for me. Despite the fact that I rarely cooked for myself, I was quite capable when given the funds and the opportunity.

Still in a daydream about making a rib roast with pearl onions, carrots, and roasted fingerling potatoes, my first table was seated. Of all people, the party included the mayor's friend Tami Lynn Carroll, surrounded by six men I pegged for foreign businessmen. I chewed the nub of a fingernail, contemplating whether I should ask her if she had suggested to the police I'd had an altercation with the mayor.

"Emmett, please take Table Five. I don't know what to say to her about the mayor," I begged. "She might be the person who told the police it was me that murdered him."

"Sorry, but no can do. My call party just got seated, and it's an eight top," Emmett said. With a wave, he swaggered off to his table.

I looked around to see if anyone else could take the table, but all the other servers hustled with tables of their own. I bit my lower lip and tried to psych myself into believing my night would be okay as I ambled over to her table. "It will be okay. As long as I don't drop anything, maybe she won't even notice me," I whispered to myself.

"Good evening, my name is Jayne, and I'll be your server," I said. I stood opposite Tami to keep an eye on her for any reaction about my presence and the mayor.

Tami Lynn smiled innocently at me, "We'll start with a magnum of the Duckhorn cabernet, please." Dismissing me, she turned to the man seated next to her and whispered something into his ear.

Maybe I did have a concussion and I'm now suffering hallucinations. What the heck was going on with this woman? How could she appear so calm when her boyfriend—or whatever the mayor was to her—had just been murdered? She certainly wasn't dressed for mourning. Her ruby red dress strained at the seams, and her breasts came perilously close to escaping. In fact, I contemplated setting another place at the table for them. Then it occurred to me maybe she didn't know about the mayor's death yet. I surely didn't want to be the person to tell her.

The rest of the night proceeded normally, except for

each time the party at Tami Lynn's table required my presence. Her smiles gave me the creeps, and something seemed off in the way she kept her eyes trained on me.

As I ran her credit card at the register, I saw her coming out of the ladies room. My conundrum... should I, or should I not, say anything to her about the mayor's death. If she didn't know about it, maybe they weren't as close as I suspected. But, if she did know, how could she go about her business as if nothing had happened?

Good sense prevailed, and I decided to simply slip a note in with her credit card expressing my condolences. I scribbled just one short sentence, "*Sorry to hear about the Mayor.*"

Tami Lynn gave me a strange glance as she and her party left, but didn't say anything about my note. Maybe I was right and she hadn't heard. After all, I didn't think it had yet hit the local news stations.

Finally, the evening came to an end. When Peter announced I won the bottle of wine, the stress of seeing Tami Lynn had left me too exhausted to care. I took my prize and headed out to the parking lot, looking forward to the next day off.

I stood in the lot for a few minutes trying to remember where I parked. My car was missing. Who would steal Betsy? Then, I remembered the miniature car. I half expected to open the door and see fifteen clowns pile out. No matter what, it would get me around until I could get my faithful car back on the road.

On a whim, I stopped off at One Eyed Jack's. It was the first place I made friends when I moved to the Valley of the Sun, and my favorite country music hangout. It wouldn't hurt to stop by for one quick drink, even if I could barely keep my eyes open. I needed to be surrounded by light-hearted people, and maybe my nerves kept me from rushing home in the dark. Thoughts of my last encounter with the mayor and his untimely and violent death kept flittering through my mind.

I parked my shiny rental car in the first spot next to the three pole corral in which two horses stood with their saddles on but girths loosen. Had I planned to stop by here, I might have snuck a carrot or two from the kitchen for just this situation. As it was, they would have to settle for some scratches behind their ears.

I stepped out of the car and was enveloped in the smell of leather, trail dust, sweaty horse and of course, horse droppings. I inhaled deeply and felt the stiffness in my shoulders release. The chestnut dunked his muzzle into the metal water trough and slurped two gallons of water in a matter of seconds. I reached between the metal poles and rubbed the white patch on his forehead between his thoughtful brown eyes.

I walked through the heavy alder doors and stepped back in time to when Arizona was still a territory. Cobwebs hung from smoke coated walls and peanut shells littered the scratched pine floor. Names of lovers were carved into the top of the bar, some crossed out and replaced with others. Dusty cowboy boots with holes in the soles dangled from the ceiling as testament to a hard life, and photos of the pro rodeo cowboys who downed a few beers here, decorated the walls. I couldn't have decorated the place better myself.

Jack's hummed with the local Sunday-night crowd who took dance lessons and stayed for the band. I took a stool in the back corner of the bar. Couples gazed adoringly into each other's eyes as they two-stepped around the sawdust-covered dance floor. The band was playing my favorite sad country love song, *When I Call Your Name.*

Tonight, even Jack's wasn't going to shake my mood. Seeing people enjoying themselves reminded me how quickly it could all end. Thoughts of the last time I'd seen the mayor played through my head like a never ending buffet of bad choices. If I hadn't locked my purse in the car I wouldn't have been alone in the house with him. If I had simply called a cab right away maybe he would still be alive. If I had let him drive me home maybe he wouldn't have been murdered.

I grabbed my purse and left before ordering a drink.

This wasn't where I needed to be tonight. I needed to feel safe and comforted in my little apartment, surrounded by my few possessions and some chocolate. I needed to squeeze my kitty tightly and hear his soft purr. A thought tugged at the edge of my subconscious as I walked through the dimly lit parking lot to my car. The murderer was still out there and could have been watching my run in with the mayor. What if I was next?

CHAPTER SIX

Monday morning came early, as it always has a way of doing. Despite my best plans to sleep in until at least nine-thirty, Bugsy had other ideas. Once awake, I vowed today would be a better day, and I would have fun preparing for my dinner with Jonas. Dragging my well-worn grandmother's cookbooks out, I sat at the kitchen counter and flipped through recipes. How to make something extra special, but still keep my budget in mind? The good news was Jonas had already seen my apartment in its earthquake-aftershock style so there wasn't any point in doing major clean up. Besides, if the meal didn't take his mind off the mess, I hoped my company would.

I found the perfect recipe, made my shopping list, and opened my mail, which lay on the counter taunting me.

Bills, bills, bills. No surprises. Cautiously, I flipped open my checkbook to calculate what could be paid now and what might have to wait. Counting in my tips from the last two nights, I realized I was missing cash. I counted it again to be sure, and remembered my apron left at the mayor's house. Its pocket held my wages for the night, as well as that "something extra" from Tami Lynn. With a little luck, it could pay my bills, buy a few things for dinner, and even keep that new kitty condo on order for Bugsy.

I dressed quickly in shorts and a t-shirt, slipped on my worn flip-flops, and jumped in the mini car to head back over to the mayor's house. This time I wouldn't leave without my apron.

For kicks, I entered the mayor's address in the rental's navigation system. Fifteen minutes later, I pulled up in front of his house, startled to see the security gate open. At least I wouldn't need to climb over again. I felt relieved to find no cars in the driveway. If I encountered the police, they might not believe I simply wanted to retrieve my apron.

I gave myself a pep talk. There is no one here and nothing to be afraid of. Bugsy needs his new kitty condo, I need to pay my bills and, darn it, I earned those tips. Just a quick in and out, and I would be on my way.

Parking as close to the back entrance as possible, I reluctantly forced myself out of the car. This time, I avoided the oleander and headed directly for the patio door. I made a deal with myself. If it's unlocked, I will grab my apron and be off in two minutes. If it's locked, I will turn around and never come back, tips be darned.

Unlocked! Today would be a good day. My flip-flops made loud slapping noises on the tile floors, emphasizing the eerie quiet in the rest of the house. Standing in the kitchen forced me to relive my last moments spent here. There, the cocktail glass shattered against the wall. Here's where we struggled and I knocked the platter to the floor. Over there, I reached for the phone and he ripped my shirt. Someone had swept up all of the broken glass, but dark smudges remained on the countertops. Upon closer examination, these revealed fingerprints. I gazed at my hands wondering if I pressed my fingers into the dust if they would match.

Gathering my wits, I searched the kitchen for my apron. It wasn't on the stools, where I thought I left it, or on the countertop. Perhaps the housekeeper put it in the laundry. I had no choice but to search the rest of the house. After coming this far, I figured I might as well throw my rope and see what I caught.

I tiptoed up the curved staircase to the second floor. I found guest bedrooms in addition to the master suite. The rooms appeared in good order, and I didn't find a laundry room or any sign of my apron. I resisted the urge to open dresser drawers, but did peek into the master-bedroom closet. Not that I expected to find my apron hanging next to the Brooks Brothers suits, but you never know.

I did a cursory examination of each room on the main floor, walking the long hallway lined on each side by western artwork. I encountered a closed door at the end of the hall, and hesitated for a moment before turning the knob. I had been strolling around like I owned the place, forgetting for a moment someone was murdered in this very house. Reality dawned. Except for the black powder on the countertop, the house seemed ordinary and not at all as if a murder had occurred here only days before.

I took a deep breath and, with a trembling hand, pushed open the heavy alder door. A massive mahogany desk and a floor-to-ceiling bookcase lined one entire wall. A spacious window allowed natural light to enter from the landscaped front yard. It struck me as odd to see no chair behind the desk.

I stepped cautiously into the room and walked toward the desk. It was one of those moments when you know you shouldn't watch the scary part of the movie, but you can't stop yourself. My legs propelled me forward, on automatic pilot.

"You know why there's no chair behind the desk," my inner chicken screamed. "Don't go over there!" But, curious Jayne yelled just as loudly in a voice straight from *The Exorcist*, "Go over there! You have to see for yourself." So, I kept walking.

Sure enough, the chicken side of me was right. The pattern of blood stains on the floor showed where the chair once stood, and even though they removed the carpet, blood had seeped to the subfloor. I gave an involuntary gasp and stepped back, leaning against the coolness of the window to regain my composure.

The mayor was a blackmailer, stole from the shelter fund, and almost raped me, but I felt sad at his death. No one should die like this. I wondered if anyone in his life would mourn him. Certainly not Tami Lynn, flirting with every man at the cocktail party and moving on with a business-as-usual attitude. In my wanderings around the house, I had found no photos of smiling family members, no evidence of happy times in his life. He may have died as he lived... alone and miserable, surrounded only by his expensive things. No, wait, he hadn't been alone. Someone, with him that night, murdered him.

Were the police any closer to finding out the killer's identity? They couldn't really suspect little old me. I was at the house that night admittedly, and probably the last person to leave the party. I did have a bit of a run-in with the mayor, not to mention that little part about me slashing at him with a knife. Not enough reason to accuse me, surely. At least I hoped it wasn't.

I was already in the house and, with no one else around, I might as well do a little of my own snooping. My goal was to find my apron with my tips. If I happened across something else that might help, all the better. Nothing beats a failure like a try, so how could I let this opportunity pass? To be honest, maybe a little part of me wanted to solve the crime and be a hero.

I couldn't bring myself to step on the blood-stained section of the floor, so I leaned across it and rested my left hand on the desk, pulling open the center drawer with my right. I shuffled through bills for his cell phone, electricity, and gym membership. Shifting to rest on my right hand, I pulled open the drawers down the left side. I found only a few empty hanging file folders and some receipts for expenses. Repeating the process on the right side I found nothing more. The police apparently looked through his desk for evidence. If they found anything substantial, they probably took it as evidence.

The crunch of gravel under tires caused me to whip around. To my horror, I saw the black Hummer at the end of the driveway. If I didn't move quickly, I would be in full view of the driver. With seconds to react, I ducked under the desk.

My heart beat so hard against my ribcage I thought it

would burst. I silently expressed gratitude for the mayor's love of the extreme... the large desk allowed me to fold my long legs and squash myself far enough underneath so my feet didn't hang out. I prayed the person would simply knock at the door, find no one home, and leave quickly. Silently, I cursed myself for my stupidity. Why didn't I leave when I didn't find my apron in the kitchen?

To my complete dismay, the person didn't even bother knocking. Instead, the front door creaked slowly open, and footsteps followed. I won the lottery when I decided to park in the back this time.

Damn, he/she/it was coming down the hallway! *I promise to be a better person. I promise I won't swear when my guests don't tip me. I promise to exercise daily and lay off the junk food.* I would willingly promise *anything* at the moment to avoid being found. I fought the urge to lose my breakfast or pee my pants.

The footsteps continued in slow deliberate steps, growing louder as the person neared. I closed my eyes and held my breath. The footsteps stopped outside the office for what surely spanned my entire lifetime, then turned and click-clacked back down the hall.

I opened my eyes and let out a ragged breath. I could hear whomever it was going up the stairs to the second floor. Now or never. As I began to crawl out from under the desk, my hair caught, so I yanked it and kept moving. Right now, I didn't care if I ripped a bald spot the size of a salad plate, as long as I could escape.

I took off my flip-flops and ran, bouncing off the wall as I turned the hallway into the kitchen, and through the house to the back door. I had to get out of here before whoever was in that Hummer came to finish me off. Not stopping long enough to close the patio door behind me, I flew to the compact. Sliding into the driver's seat, I reached to turn the key, but there was no key. Holy forking luck! Out of habit, I took it with me into the house. Should I hurry back into the kitchen, or leave on foot? With only seconds to decide, I figured the better option was to try to grab the key, rather than go up against a four-ton Hummer on foot.

Flip flops still in my hand, with my legs quivering, I ran back to the house. I slammed to a stop just outside the patio door, I listened for anyone coming down the stairs. Not hearing anything, I inched into the kitchen, my mind racing to remember where I left the keys. If walking into my apartment, I would drop my keys in a bowl on the counter. Spying them by the pantry, I started across the kitchen just as footsteps sounded on the stairs.

Without another moment's hesitation, I ducked into the walk-in pantry, assuming it was relatively safe unless the Hummer Person decided to make lunch. There on the shelf lay my apron. Mission accomplished. Now, if I could get out of here alive, I would never come within fifty miles of this house of horrors again.

I heard footsteps from the other side of the door and tried to keep from hyperventilating. Had he noticed the open back patio door? The footsteps grew softer as the person left the kitchen and headed down the hallway.

Holding my breath, I wasn't sure if I should make a break for it now, or wait to see if the person left. I counted to ten in my head to try to slow my heart rate and think clearly. Again the footsteps came down the hallway, but turned and I could hear the footfalls clumping back up the stairs. The person upstairs started opening and closing drawers, obviously searching for something.

My chance to make a run for it. I quietly opened the pantry door just enough to peek out and make sure there wasn't someone else standing guard in the kitchen. Seeing no one, I grabbed my apron, and barreled through the kitchen.

As I reached the patio door, a loud squeak sounded from the stairway. He was coming downstairs already? I dropped a shoe in my hurry to reach the car before Hummer Man could attack me.

This time, in my desperation, I did a nosedive over the hood and landed on my butt next to the driver's side door. Scrambling up, I yanked open the door, slammed down the power door lock, and turned the key. Thank goodness for a newer model that started on the first try. I threw the car in drive and smashed down the gas pedal. For a second, the clown car couldn't get traction in the gravel drive, but then we sped off, albeit in the wrong direction. At least we were headed forward and away from the house. I skidded around the driveway and into a grassy area set up as a putting green. I ran over a rose bush, and managed to get turned around and back on the driveway heading toward the road. I chanced a look in my rear-view mirror, but didn't see anyone running after me, or the Hummer in motion.

Sweat poured into my eyes, and my legs trembled so violently I could barely keep my bare foot pressed on the gas pedal. I didn't slow down until I put miles between me and that house. Once back in the relative safety of my apartment, I checked the doors and windows. No need to tempt fate anymore.

Collapsing onto my worn sofa, I took a minute to review what just happened and try to still my shattered nerves. I suppose I could have been accused of breaking and entering, but I didn't break anything to get in the house or while I was there. In itself, that should have earned me a free pass.

Pulling the clasp from my ponytail, I reached up to find something tangled in my hair. A small piece of plastic about the size of a stick of gum must have been what caught my hair during the escape from under the desk. I turned it over in my hands and tried to figure out what it was, but I had never seen anything like it. I gave up and checked my apron pockets for my tip envelope.

I found not only my tips, but a small key with a logo on the side. Perhaps the housekeeper thought it was mine and slipped it in the pocket when she put away my apron. No way did I plan to go back to the mayor's house to return it. I tossed it on the table with the plastic stick of gum, and opened the envelope.

Tami Lynn had been more than generous. Inside, I discovered three, crisp, one-hundred-dollar bills. Not enough to make me forget what happened after the party, but definitely enough to relieve some of my financial pressures.

My stomach growled, reminding me I hadn't eaten in a while and Jonas was due for dinner in a few short hours. I still had to dash off to the store, start dinner and find something suitable to wear. Part of me regretted the decision to invite him over. After the chaotic last few days, I didn't know if I was capable of making polite conversation, even if I did find him mouth wateringly handsome. Or, maybe because he *was*, my anxiety kicked up another notch.

My good manners wouldn't allow me to call him and cancel another dinner date, so I had no choice but to suck it up and move forward. I grabbed my third Diet Mountain Dew of the day and a frozen Snickers from the freezer for lunch, and dragged myself back out the door to do my errands. For once, with enough cash, I bought all of the ingredients I needed at the store, and even splurged on a few extras.

By the time Jonas arrived, the apartment had undergone a major overhaul. Basically, I just threw all the clothes and miscellaneous odds and ends into the bedroom and closed the door. I crammed the dirty dishes into the dishwasher, and picked up Bugsy's toys. Fresh flowers on my small café table and a few scented candles gave the place a nice homey feel. I safely tucked away my anxiety from the earlier encounter with the Hummer Man into a corner of my mind, and the butterflies jumbling my stomach I chalked up to first-date jitters.

He knocked on my door at exactly six-thirty, just as I pulled the roast from the oven to let it rest. I opened the door to see him leaning against the frame and holding a small bouquet of daisies.

"Well, darlin', you look better than the last time I saw you." He proffered the bouquet.

I giggled like a silly schoolgirl, and couldn't resist doing a twirl in my favorite sundress. "I'm so glad you approve." I took the bouquet and ushered him in.

"Something sure smells good." Jonas looked around the small living room/kitchen combination. "Looks better in here, too. You've been a busy girl today."

"You don't know the half of it." I was dying to tell someone about my day but, for a change, I held back. I had already exposed Jonas to enough craziness from me. Instead, I held up the bottle of wine I won at the restaurant.

"Would you like a glass of wine? Or maybe a beer? I didn't know what you liked so I have both." Whenever I was nervous around people, I started chattering like a Chihuahua on crack. Silently, I chided myself to shut up.

"Wine would be nice." He settled himself on the sofa and, before I could say to beware of the cat, Bugsy settled himself on the man's lap.

"He's a friendly little guy," Jonas said as he scratched Bugsy under the chin.

"He loves people, but he can get a little bossy, so don't say I didn't warn you."

I poured two large glasses of wine since I needed something to calm my nerves and I didn't want to look like a lush. Better to shine as a generous hostess.

I raised my glass in a toast, "May your belly never grumble, may your heart never ache, may your horse never stumble, may your cinch never break."

Jonas burst out laughing and we clinked glasses.

Alright, this night was getting off to a really good start.

For the next two hours we talked non-stop about family and work, and even a little about our past relationships. He was the oldest of three boys, his parents still lived in the house he grew up in, in Prescott an hour north of Cave Creek. He started his own business in the Valley doing home repairs and general construction, and was finally able to put a little money aside on a regular basis. He was married once, but ended it when he found his wife in bed with his youngest brother. He hadn't spoken to either of them since. It went without saying that the situation made him lose trust in women.

I shared my similar catastrophic relationship story, but left out the part about it being my only real relationship, and how, since then, I shied away from going on more than two dates with anyone. I danced around the topic of my family, not wanting to dredge up the memories of my father's death on a night when I felt truly happy for the first time in a while. I filled him in on the basics: the novelty of growing up an only child, and my somewhat precarious relationship with my mother. Jonas already knew what I did, but he laughed until he snorted at some of my stories from the restaurant.

"That was delicious," Jonas said as he helped me clear the dishes. He even offered to dry while I washed, making me wonder if he was real or an illusion.

"Would you like some dessert? I made a batch of brownies and we could finish our wine on the patio."

"Homemade brownies, too? You're a girl after my heart."

I laughed, "It's my mother's recipe, and it won a blue ribbon once at the county fair, so I think you'll like them."

Feeling suddenly shy, I grabbed the container of brownies and refilled our wine glasses. As we walked the few steps to my patio, the butterflies returned to my now full stomach, and a drop of sweat rolled down my neck despite my light dress. I wondered if he thought I invited him to spend the night and, if so, how would I tell him no. Did I even want to tell him no? It had been so long since I even felt like I wanted to be this close to a man, and now I wasn't sure I knew what to do.

Jonas opened the patio door for me, and we settled ourselves on my wicker loveseat... another lucky purchase from Goodwill. I held out the plastic container and we both leaned in to make our selection. Our gazes locked, and a lifetime passed. Our faces moved so close, I could have fallen into his deep-blue eyes. I licked my lips in anticipation of a kiss instead of chocolate, which was a change for me. I closed my eyes and leaned closer, expecting to feel his soft lips on mine. Instead, I felt a rush of wetness as I tipped my wineglass over us both.

Jonas yelped and jumped up, sending the brownies flying across the patio floor. I kept my eyes closed because I already knew what came next. Jonas would leave, turned off by my clumsiness. I would pick up the mess, more than likely eat the brownies anyway, and I would never see him again.

He surprised me by laughing.

I opened my eyes to survey the damage. "I guess you won't be tasting my blue ribbon brownies after all."

Red wine soaked the front of his shirt, following the pattern of his muscular chest, and pooled in his crotch area, but those gorgeous eyes crinkled with laughter as he looked down at himself.

"Your shirt will be ruined!" I exclaimed as I started to unbutton it. "You may be surprised to learn this, but I'm a pro at stain cleaning."

"Actually I'm not surprised by that at all, having already seen you looking pretty much like this." Jonas grasped my hands in his to stop me before I reached the last button just above the top of his tight jeans. "Maybe you better let me handle this."

I stepped back, but couldn't pry my gaze from the front of his jeans.

Following my gaze, Jonas suggested, "If you have a towel, I could try to dry off my jeans. Unless you want me to take them off, too?"

"Uh, maybe I better grab a towel."

I ran to the bathroom and routed through my towels to find one presentable enough for a guest. I tossed his shirt in the sink, leaving the water running on cold. As Jonas attempted to dry off his pants and I scrubbed the wine stain from his shirt, a loud rap sounded on my door.

I looked through the peephole to see two uniformed police officers looking as if they were on a mission.

My first reaction was to pretend I wasn't home, but Jonas called out from the kitchen asking who it was.

Confused, I opened the door. "Officers are we making too much noise?"

"Jayne Stanford?" The burlier of the two officers asked as he stood with a hand resting on his heavy gun belt.

"Yes, that's me." I raised my hand as if called upon in class to recite the answers to the homework I never did.

"Please come with us. You're under arrest for the murder of Franklin McArthur."

CHAPTER SEVEN

"Are you serious?" I tried to peek around them to see if Emmett stood there enjoying a practical joke at my expense.

"You can come along nicely or we can do this another way." He stepped closer to me, and his partner's radio squawked something about a suspect and custody.

My knees locked and my feet froze to the spot. Unable move or speak, I looked around helplessly.

"What's this about officer? Jonas's voice came from what seemed like a long distance away.

"Miss Stanford needs to come with us down to the station," the officer replied, puffing himself up and unsnapping his holster.

"Is she under arrest?"

"Are you her husband or her lawyer?"

"Neither."

"Then I would advise you to step back and mind your own business. Or, you win a free trip to hotel Maricopa County."

The other officer stepped forward, "I have a warrant for your arrest for the murder of Franklin McArthur. Ma'am, you need to come with me now."

His lips kept moving, but I couldn't hear the words over the rushing of the blood through my head. I squeezed my eyes shut, shook my head, then opened them again to see the police officers still standing in my doorway.

"Do you understand these rights?" he asked me again.

The first officer stepped closer and reached out to grasp my arm. Instinctively, I pulled away, and in the blink of an eye I found myself face down on the floor with my arms yanked behind me.

"I tried to do this nicely, but since you don't want to cooperate, we'll have to do it the hard way." He pulled me up by my arms and half led, half dragged me out the front door stuffing me into the back seat. As we drove away, my last vision was of Jonas standing shirtless with his mouth hanging open in stunned silence.

In my life, I never before enjoyed the discomfort of the back of a patrol car, nor suffered an accusation of murder, and I truly could have missed both of these firsts.

At the station, the officers fingerprinted me, took my mug shots, and shoved me into a small interrogation room. I couldn't stop chewing on my nails, or keep my legs from shaking.

After what seemed like an eternity, the door opened and Detective Stewart strode in, looking as crisp and fresh as if it were nine in the morning, rather than the evening. "Miss Stanford, we meet again." He leaned over the table toward me, and dropped a thick folder down with a thump.

"Are you ready to tell me what happened between you and the mayor on Friday night?" He inquired.

"W-what?"

"Why did you kill him?"

"What?" I said, again unable to come up with a better response. "Why would I want to kill him?"

"We know you spent the night at the mayor's house on Friday night. Was it a lover's quarrel?"

An explosion happened inside my skull while I tried to process the information and make sense of what he was saying.

"I think I may need a lawyer," I said shakily.

"You'll be permitted to make a phone call, but this will go easier on you if you talk to me now. I'll make sure the prosecutor hears your side of the story."

"There is no story. I didn't kill him. He tried to molest me, but I got away. Ask his girlfriend, she was there. At least I think she was passed out in a room somewhere. But, maybe not. I don't understand what's happening." I was rambling.

"Is that why you stabbed him with the knife? Did you wait until he passed out and then stab him? The medical examiner only found one scratch on his arm and no other defensive wounds, which may be explained by the level of alcohol in his body. You were serving the mayor drinks that evening. Did you make sure he was fully intoxicated so you could carry out your plans? There's an eyewitness who confirms your car was there all night, and she heard you arguing," Detective Stewart said.

"I locked my keys in the car, and the next morning I went back to pick it up. I told you all of this already."

"This isn't my first rodeo, lady. There was no girlfriend. No one else in the house but you and the mayor."

"You can ask my friend Emmett. He drove me over there to get my car in the morning."

"So, at some point after stabbing the mayor, you went home to set up your alibi."

The interrogation continued along those lines, and after an hour of my denials and the detective's insistence that I had murdered the mayor, I remembered an old cowboy saying, "Never miss a good chance to shut up." I figured I better follow that advice and stop flapping my jaw and digging a deeper hole than the one I'd already dug.

I made my one phone call, leaving a message on Bailey's voice mail. I still wore my pretty little sundress, as they transported me to the Maricopa County Jail to sit until my arraignment and bail hearing the next day. Not how I planned the night to end.

Between Bailey and Emmett, they would certainly get matters settled. This was all a colossal misunderstanding, and I would be released as soon as it was straightened out. Unfortunately, there was a lot I didn't know.

I cringed when they made me surrender my clothes for the jail issue black-and-white striped uniform with "Sheriff's Inmate" stamped on it in large letters. Not to mention the atrocious pink underwear. I felt itchy and dirty as I pondered how many other women had worn this same underwear before me.

They crammed me into a temporary holding cell with fifteen other yet-to-be-arraigned women. Finding an unoccupied area of floor in the back corner, I sat down cinching my long legs tightly to my chest. I hoped no one would notice my shaking hands, hear my ragged breathing, or smell the paralyzing fear that seeped from my every pore.

Too many thoughts collided in my brain, and I

couldn't isolate the pieces. I felt as if I was missing a vital piece of the puzzle, but I couldn't induce my brain to focus. I could almost smell my brain cells frying like eggs on a griddle.

If I couldn't physically get out of the cell, I figured I could at least try to remove myself mentally. The only way I would be able to prevent a full-on freak out was to find my happy place. An argument on the far side of the holding cell ensured I would remain in my current reality.

After a while, they shuffled us a few at a time, like cows through a chute, into yet another holding cell. By this time, it was getting late and it started to dawn on me that I was actually going to spend the night in jail. My arraignment would take place sometime the next day, and I wished it would be early. Finally, the guard came to take me to my cell. Despite the sweat running down between my shoulder blades, I felt a chill through my whole body.

Time seemed to move in super slow motion as we marched down the hall, execution style. With each step it was harder to move my feet as if I walked through wet cement. As the door to my cell clanged open, I knew it was too late for any attempt at bravery. I closed my eyes and prayed I wouldn't have a cellmate for my slumber party. Unfortunately, this prayer wouldn't be answered.

"In you go," said the guard, giving me a nudge.

My legs locked and a slight breeze fanned me as the

door slammed shut.

"Come on in, honey," said a deep voice from the bottom bunk.

I stood staring at the exposed toilet, metal sink, and the twin metal bunks attached to the wall, and shut my eyes tight as the tears poured down my face.

"A first timer I see. Don't worry, I won't bite ya, and I don't even have head lice," she said with throaty laugh. "What's your name, doll?"

"Jayne. What's yours?" I asked, too afraid to look her way.

"Folks know me as Kiki."

"Nice to meet you, Kiki," I squeaked remembering my manners.

"You've got the top bunk." Kiki pointed to the thin, worn mattress perched atop a metal bed frame.

I looked at the bunk and, before I could say another word, ran to the toilet and threw up until there was nothing but bile left in my stomach. Cupping my hand under the faucet, I rinsed my mouth with the rusty-tasting water, and climbed up onto my bunk. The coarse blanket smelled worse than wet dog, but I pulled it over my head anyway.

Kiki rapped on the side of my bed, "You're not going to be doing that all night are you?"

"No, I don't think I have anything left. I've never

been in jail before."

"No shit. I would have never guessed."

I continued hiding under the stiff blanket, which reeked of body odor, afraid to acknowledge I was really in a cell. The cacophony of sounds reminded me of the restaurant dishwasher on a busy Saturday night, banging pots and pans in his haste to keep up. Not only sounds threatened to overwhelm me, but also the smells. As a server, I fine-tuned my sense of smell to pick out the various herbs and seasonings used in the recipes without ever asking the chef. Here, my nostrils burned with the strong smell of urine and vomit. It enveloped me, threatening my gag reflex again.

Kiki yanked my security blanket off. "Come out of there. I won't be able to sleep all night if you're whimpering like a lost puppy."

I rolled over on my side and came eye to eye with my cellmate. Kiki had short spikey blonde hair, the largest breasts I had ever seen, and stood at least six feet tall. Reluctantly, I sat up on my bunk, legs dangling over the side.

"What's your story?" Kiki asked.

"They say I killed the mayor of Cave Creek. But, I'm innocent." I slid off the bunk to stand beside her.

"Yeah, that's what we all say." Kiki shook her head. "Was he the one who gave you that shiner?"

I touched my face. In all the turmoil, I forgot about

my black eye. "No, I got that from a car accident. Someone ran me off the road. What about you? Have you ever been arrested before?" I asked.

"Oh, I'm in here whenever I need a vacation." She chuckled.

"Huh?"

"Every now and then, I get nabbed with a client, and the vice guys give me a little vacation of sorts. Get a day off, rest up a bit, and finally my boss gets the charges dropped. Then, it's back to work," she said.

"You mean you're a hooker?" I asked, not quite sure I followed the discussion correctly.

She laughed again. "Sugar, classy ladies like myself are called escorts. Haven't gotten around much, have you?"

"Do you work for a pimp or something?"

"I got a guy who handles the business end and sets up the dates but, after that, it's all me. I'm not your typical date, as you can tell." Kiki strutted around our eight-by-eight-foot cell. "I don't go in for too much kinky stuff, but I have a following. My real job is as a celebrity impersonator. You should drop by and catch my show over at the Lone Star Casino."

I really wanted to ask Kiki about what it was like to be an escort and if the money was as good as I'd heard. My pause button kicked in. "You should come and see me, too.

I'm a server at Wild Bronco up in Cave Creek."

Kiki continued without missing a beat, "So, you knocked off the mayor? What'd he do?"

"He was stabbed but, honestly, I didn't do it." Even I was getting tired of hearing me say the same words again and again.

"My old man used to slap me around a bit. Finally got out and took my kid with me. Tough raising a kid by myself, but better than having him start on her next," Kiki said. "It's lights out soon, so you better get comfortable. You aren't going anyplace tonight, girlfriend."

Kiki stripped down to her jail issue underwear, and kicked back on her cot. Too embarrassed to undress or even use the toilet, I climbed back up to my bed, again drawing the blanket around me as a shield. I could hear Kiki mumbling to herself punctuated by an occasional sniffle.

"Kiki, are you okay?" I called down to her.

"I'm okay. I hate leaving my kid home alone," she said softly.

"Do you ever want to do something else besides being an escort?" I asked timidly.

"Sure, who don't? I quit school in the ninth grade, and there aren't a lot of jobs that will pay what I make. I've been on the streets since I was a girl, and this cell is like the Four Seasons Hotel compared to that. Besides my kid is in her last year of high school. She's real smart, and I know she'll go to college if I can just work a little while longer."

At that, it was lights out. The noise level dropped a few decibels, but I knew I wouldn't be sleeping tonight. Kiki started snoring within minutes, obviously enjoying her mini "vacation" to some degree, even though she missed her daughter.

Curled up into a ball, trying not to inhale the smells left by the last "guest," I tried to make my mind concentrate on happy thoughts.

Tomorrow, I was sure this misunderstanding would be cleared up and I would be able to go home. I knew the evidence pointed in my direction, but I was optimistic that they were beating the streets right now looking for the true killer. Unfortunately, the realization slammed into my brain that the police thought they already had their killer in custody, so they were probably home with the family, and not giving me a second thought.

Hiding under the cover on my cot, the memories of all of my past failures started spinning through my head like a merry-go-round I couldn't leave. How many times had I tried to do something, and wound up making a worse mess of things? This time may be the biggest failure of them all because, this time, I might actually face the death penalty.

I must have dozed off eventually because the next

thing I knew it was morning. Not that we had a window or any way to tell the time of day but, when I opened my eyes, some natural light lit up the cell block. I hopped down as quietly as I could to avoid disturbing Kiki, and tried to freshen up with the limited resources in the metal sink.

"Stanford," the jailer called loudly outside of my cell. "Time for your arraignment."

I dashed to the cell door, more than ready to bid farewell to the hotel Maricopa.

"People trying to sleep here!" Kiki yelled from her bunk.

"Bye, Kiki. I hope things work out for you. I'm sure this misunderstanding has been cleared up and I'll be released," I said as I left the cell. As an afterthought, I added, "Do you want me to check in on your daughter for you?"

Kiki rolled over in her bunk and looked at me, her eyes puffy. "I should be out of here this afternoon, but thanks for the offer."

"Stay in touch," I called as the officer led me down the hallway toward, what I hoped, was freedom.

"Yeah, sure. Let's do lunch." Kiki's laughter followed me until the metal doors slammed shut behind me.

The jailer escorted me to the courtroom for my arraignment. Bailey and Emmett sat in the back of the courtroom, and it was all I could do not to release a flood of tears when I saw them. I had cried more in the past couple of days than in the last ten years, and I wondered if I had been storing up tears.

An attorney sitting at the defendant's table advised me he had been retained by Emmett to represent me. His quivering hands dropped my file on the floor, and my short life history fluttered around as if throwing up its hands in pointlessness. When the judge asked me how I wished to plead, we stood, and I said, "Not guilty." He set my bail at $250,000 and, this time, I couldn't prevent the sobs from escaping as an officer led me back to my cell. This couldn't be happening to me.

The rest of the detainees were off eating breakfast, so my cell was empty. I almost resigned myself to life in jail until my hearing in six months, when the jailer came to tell me I made bail. I almost kissed him, but didn't want to take a chance he would change his mind and lock me away forever.

I walked out the front door of the County Jail, and there stood Bailey and Emmett.

"I'm so glad to see you both!" I exclaimed as I gripped them together in a bone-crushing hug.

Bailey looked out of place in her business skirt and jacket with sensible heels. She generously put up her house as collateral for my bail, and posted the ten percent required by the bail bondsman.

Emmett found my attorney by looking in the Yellow Pages, and it was the lawyer's first criminal case. He worked cheap, so I couldn't complain at this point, but I had a feeling I would need to do my own investigating to ensure this case didn't go any further.

"Are you okay?" Emmett asked as I leaned against them taking deep breaths of the downtown Phoenix air.

At that moment, I didn't care if the air was polluted with the exhaust of too many cars, or if the pollen count was in the danger zone. To my senses, the air carried the perfume of freedom. My every exposed pore sucked up the sunshine as if it were oxygen.

"These have been the worst few days of my life." After a second's contemplation on all the bad weeks in my life, I added, "Well, maybe the second worst."

"Come on you two, let's get out of here before they arrest us for loitering," Bailey said. She pushed us down the steps toward the street.

On the way home, sitting in the front seat of Emmett's car, I filled them in on what I knew from the detective. None of it made sense. The police had no doubt I murdered the mayor, and I was just as determined to find the proof of my innocence. Unfortunately, during the time when someone murdered mayor McArthur, I was wandering a back road trying to find my way home. Luckily, if he would still talk to me, Jonas could verify my whereabouts. He couldn't prove that I didn't murder the mayor and then hit the road, and I didn't think his testimony would be enough to prove my innocence, but I was desperate. Anything was better than nothing.

Back at my apartment, I took a steaming hot shower in an effort to wash away the stench of jail, which lingered on me like the smell of mildew on an old sponge. Emmett left, and Bailey sat at the kitchen counter perusing my junk mail when I came out of the shower.

"What are you doing with this?" She held up the plastic stick-of-gum thingy I found stuck in my hair.

"I found it, but I don't know what it is." I conveniently left out the part about me snooping around the murder victim's house, since I wasn't sure she would approve.

"It's a flash drive."

"A what?"

"You stick this end into your computer and store files or photos, whatever you want to store separately." She pushed one side, and a metal end popped out. "Where did you find this?"

"Well, it's kind of a long story."

Bailey stood with her hands on her hips and an expression I knew meant she wasn't going to drop the subject. "Jayne, we're best friends, and you can tell me anything. I know you're holding out on me." She led me over to the sofa and sat next to me holding my hands in hers.

I poured out the whole story, even the parts I hadn't told anyone.

Bailey sat dumbfounded, then pulled me in for a long hug. "You are one of a kind. I've never met anyone who could get into so much trouble without even trying, but I guess that's part of what makes you so special. You're like the much taller little sister I never had, and you know I'm here for you, no matter what."

That comment and her tears made me cry even harder, "You're like the sister I never had, too," I sobbed into her shoulder.

We regained our composure, passed the box of tissues between us and, even though it was still early afternoon, I poured us each a hefty glass of wine. I needed something to help dim my sensory overload.

"This is the wine Jonas and I drank the night I was arrested." I stared into the glass as if I could look back and relive the evening before the arrest.

"So, obviously, you haven't spoken to him since the police came. Will he verify your alibi?"

"Twice the guy has rescued me, and what happens when I try to repay him? He watches me get arrested, and almost gets himself arrested, too. My guess is he'll want to stay as far away from me as possible. Despite that, I think he's one of the good guys, and I'm pretty sure he'll tell the police what he knows. I better drive you home before I finish this glass of wine, or none of your critters will eat dinner tonight."

Bailey chugged the rest of her wine to give her the courage to get back on the road. Even with the alcohol to help relax her, she white knuckled it until I dropped her at her door. As much as I wanted to ask her about her fears, I knew tonight was not the time to push it. Each time I tried in the past, she gave a different excuse, but something in her eyes betrayed the real fear that lay deep within her. When she was ready, she would tell me what gave her such a profound fear of cars and driving. For the time being, I had enough on my mind not to pry into her past, even if I was desperate for a distraction.

After dropping her off at her house, I made a plan for the rest of my day. First thing on my agenda: contact Jonas and ask him to verify my alibi, or at least the part he knew about. After that, I had to pick up some cat food, and do laundry. Not the most glamorous super sleuth, but Bugsy must eat, and I needed clean clothes for work.

I dug through the dirty clothes on the floor to find the pants I wore the night of the cocktail party. Retrieving

Jonas' card, I dialed his number. I tried to imagine what he must think of me. After all, the man had seen me wandering in the night with ripped, dirty clothes and my hair looking like I used a vacuum cleaner for a blow dryer; rescued me from a desert wash; and seen me thrown to the floor and arrested for murder. Is it possible to make a worse impression? I hoped he was focused on the lovely dinner we had before the arrest. Either way, what did I have to lose? I needed his help again just as gravely as the first time.

He answered on the second ring, "Jonas Harper."

Darn, how could I still manage to be tongue-tied after my pep talk? Maybe it was the thought of his lips mere inches away from mine while the smell of freshly baked brownies tickled my nose.

"Hi, it's Jayne."

"Are you okay?"

"I've had better days," I admitted. "The police think I murdered the mayor, but I swear I didn't do it. You're the only person who saw me that night."

No response. I started to think he hung up on me.

"So what do you want me to do?" he finally asked.

"Can you call the police and tell them what happened?"

"I could make things worse. I feel responsible for you getting arrested the way you did. If I hadn't stepped in, you might not have wound up on the floor handcuffed."

I didn't know how to respond to that, but since my situation was approaching critical status, I needed him to vouch for me. "I don't think things can get any worse than they are right now."

"I can only tell them what I know, and not what happened before I found you."

"That would be fantastic. I owe you big time!"

"I'm sure we could find a way for you to repay me."

I'm not sure what Jonas was thinking, but my mind went directly to the gutter. Bad Jayne reared her head, and I had visions of running my fingers through his dark hair and slow sensuous kisses.

"Are you still there?" he asked.

"Ah, sorry, I was distracted for a minute. We could try dinner again. Maybe actually get through dessert."

"How about if we go out the next time? It might be safer to be in a public place."

I wasn't sure if he meant because I could potentially be a murderer, or he didn't trust himself to be alone with me. I figured I would go with the second scenario. "My next night off isn't until Sunday. How does that sound?"

"Sounds like a plan. In the meantime, I'll give the police detective a call and tell him what I know."

I gave him contact information for Detective Stewart,

and he promised to call right away. Unconsciously, I chewed my cuticle. I hoped his testimony would clear my name and this would all be behind me in a few days. If not, I could face life in prison, or worse... a slow drip into a forever sleep.

CHAPTER EIGHT

One task accomplished, I headed out to run my errands. Bailey called on my cell phone just as I pointed the mini car toward town.

"I've been playing around with that flash drive you found. I believe it belonged to the mayor since there was some generic stuff relating to the mayor's office. There were also some nasty emails between him and his ex-wife, and a few odd ones between him and that Tami Lynn Carroll lady," Bailey said.

"Can you forward those to me and I'll read them when I get home?" I asked.

"There are a few more files to go through, some of which are encrypted. I'll let you know if I find anything there. Call me later and I'll give you an update" She hung up.

I drove through my errands on autopilot, thinking about what I should do next. Multiple thoughts swirled around in my head like a desert dust devil. If the mayor and his ex-wife were quarreling about something, would it have compelled her to kill him? I would need to create a list of potential suspects.

I thought about how I solved the brain teasers my father would pose to me during our fishing outings. This problem wasn't as simple as solving an imaginary puzzle and stopping for an ice cream on the way home. If I didn't figure out this mystery I could say goodbye to everything I treasured. I picked up my work shirts from the one-dollar dry cleaners, and made a stop at the pet food store, making sure to include a new fuzzy mouse toy for Bugsy. I even grabbed a few groceries for myself: chocolate cream-filled cupcakes, a box of cereal, a twelve-pack of Diet Mountain Dew, and a box of macaroni and cheese. All of that would hold me over until I felt compelled to cook some healthy food. Not exactly the diet of champions, but my brain didn't function without my daily intake of caffeine and chocolate. The cupcakes would fill double duty as breakfast and dessert. Somewhere in the middle, I would eat the cereal and maybe even an apple if I found one rolling around my refrigerator. The macaroni and cheese would work as lunch, and I rarely ate dinner since I was usually at work.

When Bugsy was happily shredding his new toy, his stomach full and his belly rubbed, I knew he would be occupied and not even miss me for a few more hours. It excused me from any guilt trips.

The stress of this day began to hit me full force. Despite my exhaustion, I had no choice but to put on the work clothes and head off to Wild Bronco for the start of my four-thirty shift. I didn't feel like I had the energy to put on a happy face but, at the same time, familiar surroundings seemed like a good idea. The restaurant served as my home away from home, and my co-workers as my second family.

I arrived early and knew I would have ample time to prepare my station and sample the nightly specials. My stomach grumbled at the thought of it. Once again, I hadn't stopped moving long enough to eat anything, despite my junk food supplies. I walked in the back door licking my lips in anticipation. Maybe tonight I would find another chocolate cake, or a crème brulee, or the vanilla bean ice cream-filled profiteroles. Whatever it was, I planned to make sure I got a large taste.

As I walked through the kitchen fragranced with the smells of freshly baked breads, a figurative cloud passed over the sun. Chatter stopped, and all eyes focused on me.

If I was going to be the star of the evening's entertainment, I figured I might as well put on a good show. I walked behind the line to where the chefs kept the knives. Looking over the choices, I selected the biggest, sharpest knife in the collection. Pulling it out for inspection, I held it close to my face, breathed on it, then wiped it on my apron.

"Tonight, I want my orders to come out first, and there better be a piece of cake left at the end of the shift." I brandished the knife while scanning the faces of the kitchen staff to gauge their reactions.

"Oh, Jayne, you are one crazy chick," laughed Sal, the chef. "I never believed you really could have done it."

"Sal, you know I'm nothing but a big sissy."

"I promise you, I will save you something special after the shift. We'll have a drink to toast your freedom," Sal said. He took the knife from me and wiped it down. "In the meantime, I'll just hang on to this knife in case you get tempted."

"If I was going to use that, it would be to cut chocolate cake now rather than waiting until later."

I continued to the front of the house, and checked at the hostess stand to find out what section I was assigned. Oddly, my name wasn't written on any section at all. I inspected the reservation book to see if the number of reserved tables were way down. I thought perhaps Peter tried to call me off. Even though it was a Tuesday night, I saw several big parties listed... we looked busy. I flipped through numerous pages thinking it a mistake.

"Jayne, what are you doing here?" Peter asked,

coming up behind me.

"I believe I work here, unless I've totally lost my mind."

"I didn't know you were released." Peter avoided looking me in the eyes.

"I made bail. I'm free as a bird until the trial. Besides you know it wasn't me."

"I know you complain about him every time he's been here, and I had to tell the police that when they asked me," Peter said.

"You what?"

Peter shifted his weight from foot to foot. "I didn't want to get you in trouble, but they came here snooping around and got the guys in the kitchen all worried about deportation. You know some of them have creative paperwork when it comes to their legal status."

"I wish I could say thanks for all the help, but somehow I can't find the right words."

"Look, Jayne, until this is all cleared up, it doesn't look good for the restaurant to have you here."

"I'm fired?" I asked in astonishment.

"No, let's just say you're taking a short vacation." He tugged at his collar.

It was becoming hard for me to breathe, "I need this job. My rent will be due, and I was counting on this week's tips. I haven't done anything wrong!"

Peter cleared his throat. "I'm sorry, Jayne, I had to do it. I'm sure this will blow over soon, and you'll be back before you know it." He patted me on the back lightly.

I gathered my things and headed back through the kitchen with my lower lip quivering. I won't let anyone see my cry, I vowed.

"Jayney, hold up," Emmett yelled as I reached my car door.

"Emmett, I've been sent home, indefinitely. What am I going to do?" I laid my head against the roof of my miniature car.

"I could loan you a few bucks if you need it to get by," he offered.

"I couldn't take your money. I know you're not much better off than I am."

"Is there anything you want to tell me about that night?" He leaned closer.

"How could you ask me that?"

"Just checking," he said with a chuckle. "Let's try to keep you out of jail so you can pay that top-notch lawyer I found you."

"You are the biggest pain in the butt I have ever met. I changed my mind, I will take your money." A sound escaped my mouth that was more of a croak than a laugh.

"Hang in there, Jayne." Emmett gave me a quick hug. "I have to get back in there, but let me know if there's anything you need."

"You could find out who really killed the mayor," I yelled after him.

Here I was with a whole night off and nothing to do. It was not even five o'clock. I had hours to burn. I meant to turn the steering wheel toward home, but somehow the clown car headed to One Eyed Jack's.

I patted the dashboard, "You're starting to grow on me, little car. You knew what I needed even when I didn't know myself."

A cloud of arid dust danced around me as if even Mother Nature wanted to take a reprieve and kick up her heels to some good ol' country music. I ambled into the bar and took my favorite seat in the back corner where I could look out over the rest of the room. A few families sat eating an early dinner while the jukebox played Travis Tritt singing "A Modern Day Bonnie and Clyde." I loved this timeworn bar where the house band played their hearts out and you could always find a friend. In the semi-darkness, I could regroup before heading home.

"Hey, Jayne," called Gus, the long-time bartender. "What are you doing here so early on a work night?'

"I got the night off. Actually, I got the next few weeks

of nights off until the trial is over," I responded as I slouched over the bar.

"Oh, I almost forgot about the whole murder rap. You're the talk of the town." Gus leaned his elbows on the bar.

"Finally, I get my moment in the sun," I said sullenly. "Aren't you going to ask if I did it?"

Gus chuckled, "Do you want me to ask?"

"You'll be the only person who hasn't."

Rather than answering, Gus looked around the almost-empty bar while continuing to polish the glass in his hand. "I remember one rainy afternoon over a year ago when this gal wandered into Jack's. She wore this lost look on her face and sat in the same seat you're in now. She was kind of quiet at first but, before we knew it, she became a regular, and anyone who met her considered her a friend. I can't imagine that person ever doing anything to hurt someone else."

I smiled at the memory. "I just remembered why I love this place."

"What's really funny is, a line of cowboys waited out the door to get a date with this girl... even the old bartender took a shot, but she didn't have eyes for anyone."

"Oh, Gus, you're exactly what I needed tonight. Even if ninety-five percent of what you say isn't true. I don't know how I wound up with a murder hanging over my head."

Gus commiserated with me for an hour. When the bar started to fill up, I took it as my signal to head home. I wasn't feeling as betrayed at being put out to pasture as I did earlier, but chaos still ricocheted inside my head. How was I going to pay my rent, my utilities, my credit cards and, most importantly, buy cat food for Bugsy? I may have been a screw-up most of my life, but I never neglected my kitty. I would make sure he was cared for, even if I went hungry. Not only was I charged with a murder I didn't commit, but now I had lost my only source of income, and could wind up homeless. Just me and my little cat living off the land. No, that wouldn't work, I had no clue how to survive in the desert, and Bugsy was more likely to be coyote bait than a willing Boy Scout.

I drove home with more thoughts than I could handle at war in my head. Maybe instead of dealing with things I didn't want to think about, I would turn on the television, find an old movie, and shut down my brain. Pulling into my reserved spot, I dragged myself up the walk. Odd, there was no kitty waiting in the window for my return.

As I went to put my key in the lock, the door swung open to reveal a scene of mass destruction. My home had been ransacked. If it wasn't for bad luck, it didn't look like I would have any luck at all.

I couldn't propel myself beyond the threshold. I

should have felt fear, but that emotion had drained from me like the last drop of water from a canteen over the last few days. One question did sneak up on me... where was Bugsy?

He didn't come out to greet me, which only happened once before, when he accidentally locked himself in the cupboard while in search of his treats. I called out to him, but no answering meow came. The absence of Bugsy's meows made my ears hurt.

The small living room, never neat by anyone's standard, looked as if a hurricane had blown through. Sofa cushions tossed, my mother's handmade needlepoint pillows ripped open, my magazines and few books lying like sway-backed ponies. Tiptoeing over the rubble, I looked into my kitchen where the cabinets had spewed their contents as if finally disgusted with my food selections. The refrigerator door stood open, and they even emptied my box of cereal over the counter. I walked to my bedroom where the unmade bed stood buried beneath piles of clothes and every shoe I owned. Sad to say, that room looked almost the same as when I left. I felt violated. All of my meager belongings rifled through by a stranger.

Worst of all... no sign of Bugsy. In anguish, I called out his name and began tearing through the rubble, desperate to find him. I was stunned by the destruction to my apartment, but no words could describe the way I felt when I couldn't find my beloved cat. Not once did it cross my frazzled mind that my first duty should be to call the police.

I started to search, opening cupboards, my closet door, anyplace he could have been locked in. Bugsy was definitely not home.

He was a smart cat. In fact, I frequently held conversations with him in which I would swear he understood me completely. Did he run from the vandals? Did thieves take him when they couldn't find anything else of value? The front door hadn't been closed completely, so perhaps he escaped after the thieves left.

At the rate my hysteria rose, I was headed for a stroke or a complete meltdown. What else could possibly happen? Maybe someone in the complex saw him wandering around and took him in. Bugsy was a sheltered indoor cat that never ventured farther than the front door. If he got out when the vandals came in, he wouldn't know where to go or how to get back home. Despite myself, I started to cry again. When had I become such a complete baby? I should own stock in a tissue manufacturer.

Common sense finally took hold of me and I grabbed my cell phone and dialed 911.

"911, what is your emergency?"

"My cat is missing and someone broke into my apartment," I sobbed.

"Is someone in your apartment now, miss?" the operator asked.

"No, but my cat is missing. Can you send the fire department or someone to help me find him?"

"Miss, is your apartment on fire?"

"No, I uh, just need someone to help me find Bugsy."

"Is this some kind of practical joke?"

"No, my apartment was vandalized and my cat is missing." I repeated trying to calm my voice. "Can you please, please send someone to help me?"

"Okay, I'll send a unit out to your apartment. Please stay on the line with me until the officers arrive."

I did as ordered, and remained on the line with the nice lady. She talked to me in a calming voice until I could breathe regularly again.

Within minutes, lights from the squad car painted a pattern on my walls. I told the 911 Operator the police had arrived, and we disconnected.

Two patrol officers came up to the door cautiously. I wondered if they were worried about who vandalized my apartment or, when hearing my name over their radio, realized I was an accused murderer.

The lead officer walked me through the apartment to determine what besides my cat was missing. As far as I could tell, nothing had been taken. My television was an old model too heavy to move, let alone steal, and my computer desktop was from the dark ages. The only thing the police could tell for sure... there was no forced entry. They wrote up a standard police report advising me to contact my renter's insurance. I didn't even know there was such a thing, let alone have funds to pay for it.

I overheard one officer comment to his partner as they left that I was probably just a slob and this is what it always looked like. That comment resulted in guffaws at my expense.

I locked the doors behind the police and turned on every light I could, including the one over the stove. Sitting down at my little cluttered kitchen table, I missed my cat and my job, and worried about my future. I laid my head down on the cool tile tabletop and wondered what would happen to me. What else could possibly go wrong in my life? I closed my eyes and thought about the last time I saw my father alive.

We had gone out in our little rowboat to fish... a Saturday afternoon ritual. I never really liked fishing, but I would have gone, no matter what, just to spend the time with him. It was our time, and no one could ever interfere with it. An unexpected storm racing in caught us too far out on the Chesapeake Bay to make it back to shore. Our small fishing boat capsized and I wore the only life jacket. I tried to save my Dad, but I was only twelve and scared. I believed my mother always blamed me for his death, because nothing was ever the same between us after that fateful day.

Thinking back, it occurred to me now, that maybe I cut my mother out of my life because I couldn't stand myself. Just maybe, I judged her too harshly all these years. It was possible that all the time I thought she was judging me, it was really me judging myself. Maybe I shouldered the blame of his death because I couldn't come up with any other valid argument for him to be taken from me.

Lifting my head, and taking a deep breath, I looked around the room. The apartment remained in disarray, but honestly I was accustomed to that situation by my own hand. Nothing mattered more to me than my four-legged best friend. He needed me, and I couldn't save him if I couldn't crawl out of this situation.

I knew I should call Bailey or Emmett, or even Jonas, but I couldn't allow them to rescue me again. No matter where else I failed, I realized this was one task I must see through to the end. I was compelled to find out who killed the mayor and clear my name. My stomach ached at the challenge, but I steeled myself to do whatever it took. I would toughen up. If this was a test, I better figure out a way to pass it. And soon!

CHAPTER NINE

I wish I could blame this mess of a life on someone else. I managed to get myself into this, and somehow I would find my way out. I just hoped I wouldn't have to do it from behind prison bars.

Sitting down at my computer, I read through the emails Bailey forwarded to me from the mayor's flash drive. It looked to me like Evangeline McArthur had several reasons to want him dead. The rumor mill said her ex-husband had unscrupulously milked her of all of her inheritance and, when the money evaporated, divorced her. Reading her emails, it seemed that small-town gossip carried some truth behind it.

I decided to run a search on the Internet to see what else I could find out about the ex-Mrs. McArthur.

Dozens of hits came up with her name, many with photos of her and the infamous Franklin during an earlier time in the relationship. Evangeline was a striking woman with a willowy figure, fifteen years older than her husband. Her late father was a highly successful local businessman with a sterling reputation. As his only heir, she inherited everything, including the furniture stores, which created his fortune. She was living the dream life when Franklin came into town as an aspiring politician.

Evangeline looked smitten in the first photos of the two of them. As soon as they married, she turned over the full responsibility of the stores and named him as the new president. The reports showed, in three years, the businesses her father had nurtured for fifty years all filed bankruptcy. Franklin McArthur was elected mayor and walked away, leaving her bankrupt and broken hearted. The news reports included some allegations of physical abuse and drugs, but no charges were ever pressed.

By the end of the marriage, she lost her beautiful estate in Carefree, her Mercedes automobiles, her fine clothes and jewelry. She lived in a small one-bedroom condo, alone but for her one friend, an old cockatoo. Abandoned by her high-society friends as quickly as the money disappeared, I guessed she clung to a lot of anger about her ex-husband.

Reading every story I found online about the ex-Mrs. McArthur depressed me. My eyes burned from staring at the computer screen, my entire body ached and, despite the increasingly loud growls coming from my stomach, the thought of eating repulsed me. The situation is serious when even chocolate won't help. With nothing left for me to do, I crawled into bed and pulled the covers over my head. I hoped sleep would give me a reprieve from my life.

The next morning, I awoke early... odd considering my four-footed wakeup call wasn't there to place his breakfast order. Maybe the quiet of the room caused my eyes to pop open at first light. My subconscious must have registered the lack of the fifteen-pound lump hogging half the bed, and the hole in my life the little furry bundle left when he went missing. I crawled out of bed and turned on the computer.

I was a whiz on the point of sale terminal at the restaurant, largely due to the orders I rang incorrectly for a long time after I started. If I were allowed to call out my orders to the kitchen, I would never have a problem. I could easily recall every order with every menu change, and balance that with multiple drink requests. I sometimes relished taunting Emmett with this skill since it was the one thing I did better than him.

My home computer was a horse of a different color. It intimidated me with all its burps and screen savers, which popped up at the strangest times. Creating a missing cat flyer would be daunting, but a welcome reprieve from my other problems. For a short while I would put aside the pressing issues of no work, no pay, and a murder rap.

An hour later, and all of the change in my wallet dumped into my cuss jar, I printed out twenty copies of a flyer. A blurry picture of something that resembled a cat was shown above my name and cell phone number. I showered and, as I pulled a t-shirt out of my drawer, I came across a white whisker. I took it as a sign that I would find Bugsy, and taped it to his picture on my nightstand. I dressed quickly and debated with myself about whether I should leave the patio door open in case he came home on his own. With flyers in hand, I canvassed the neighborhood, calling his name.

Three hours later, even more distraught than when I began, I taped my last flyer to a light pole near my parking spot. I sat down on the curb with my head in my hands. My kitty was gone—maybe hurt, scared, or thirsty—and there was no doubt he would be hungry. That guy never missed a meal.

"Are you all right, dear?"

I peered through my fingers to see a pair of size-six running shoes so white they nearly blinded me. My eyes moved slowly up the sky-blue polyester tracksuit to the lovely aged face topped by a short curly mass of gray hair.

"My cat is missing and he may have been eaten by a coyote."

"Is that a picture of your kitty?" she asked pointing to

the flyer.

"Yes, have you seen him?"

"I don't think so. When did you lose him?"

I stood on wobbly legs, "Someone broke into my apartment and he must have gotten out then."

"Oh my, that's terrible. I thought this was a safe neighborhood. What unit are you in?" She pressed her hand to her heart.

"I'm just there," I said pointing to my front door.

"We're neighbors. I live two doors down. When was your apartment broken into?"

"Last night when I was at work. Well, I wasn't actually at work, but I left for work and then they gave me the night off. Actually, they gave me more than the night off, and I have bills to pay, so I didn't come right home... but maybe if I had, this wouldn't have happened. It's all my fault," I rambled, as fresh tears trailed down my face.

"I walk the neighborhood once a day, so maybe I'll see him. What time did you say he went missing?"

"Let's see, I left here around four o'clock and got back around seven-thirty, so sometime in between someone broke into my apartment."

"That's around the time my daughter-in-law Agnes came to check on me. She's a pain, but I suppose she means well. I remember she was complaining about a large car taking up two spaces, mine included."

"Do you think that could have been the person that broke into my apartment? Did you hear anything?" I asked.

"No, but I did see the black truck thingy parked in my spot, because I walked her out when she left. Agnes was still complaining about it as she drove off."

"Are you sure it wasn't someone who lives here?"

"I've never seen it before," she said.

"It was a large black truck, like a pickup truck?"

"No, but it was one of those new things the kids drive around in these days. It looked like it could fit a family of ten."

Large and black, and outside my apartment the same night it was vandalized. Perhaps, the unexplained Hummer? For the first time, I considered that my apartment break-in might not be a random act. My instinct told me this was yet another piece to the puzzle, but what did I have worth taking? My most valuable possession, my four-legged family member, was gone. Other than my cat, my few possessions weren't worth much. But why break in and steal my cat?

I thanked my neighbor and asked her to keep her eyes open in case she saw my kitty running around the neighborhood. I needed to keep moving to feel like I was doing something productive. Now would be a good time to meet with Franklin McArthur's ex-wife to see if she had an alibi for the night he was murdered.

I spent an hour in the bathroom trying to decide how to fix my hair and makeup. I tried to envision meeting with the ex-wife of the man you're accused of killing, and I felt an odd compulsion to put my best foot forward. In the end, I opted for the hair down and a simple pair of Capri pants with a jeweled t-shirt.

Thinking I could record our conversation, I dug around on the floor looking for the contents of my kitchen drawers to try to find an old digital recorder I once used for my few college courses. Evangeline McArthur had plenty of reasons for wanting to take revenge. I wondered how she would benefit by his death other than knowing he finally got rewarded for his bad deeds. I didn't find my recorder, but did find some odd change, an old chewed up cat collar, buttons I was saving to sew on a few shirts, and a lipstick I didn't know I owned. I would keep my cell phone close at hand in case anyone called in with a Bugsy sighting.

I had a general idea of the apartment complex she lived in, but not the exact unit. I counted on luck to help me find her. My plan was to go with the surprise attack and catch her off guard.

Looking at myself in the rear-view mirror, I didn't recognize the woman staring back at me. Her jaw clenched and her eyes flashed with determination. This woman looked like she would get the job done. I might start to like this new Jayne.

Evangeline's complex was located on Sundance Trail in Carefree. Only when I pulled into the complex did I realize it was a senior living residence. The well-maintained grounds bloomed profusely with bougainvillea and oleander plants. I parked in a guest spot, taking note of several golf carts in front of the main office, surely used to ferry the residents into town for errands. I sat for a moment to think of a plan. I hadn't anticipated how I would get to her apartment once I arrived, or even what I would say... only what I would wear to the visit. One thing at a time was my motto.

Lucky for me, inspiration arrived in the form of a flower delivery. I hopped out of the compact just as the florist's driver exited the van with a large birthday bouquet complete with balloons.

"I work here. I'll take that in for you," I said trying to wrest the flowers from his hands.

"I'm supposed to deliver these to Mrs. Martha Jackson," he said fighting back.

"It's the policy that only staff can deliver flowers to the residents." I was still pulling on the vase he tightly gripped.

"I've always delivered the flowers right to their doors."

"It's a new policy to protect tenant's privacy. You know all about the new privacy laws in this State, right?" I leaned in and gave my best menacing stare.

"Oh, yeah sure." He looked around as if caught committing a crime.

"Thanks, I'll take them from here." I gathered the balloons and flowers from him.

I carried the birthday arrangement inside, trying to hide my face and still walk at the same time... no easy accomplishment considering I was generally on the losing side of feet versus Jayne.

"I have a delivery for Evangeline McArthur," I lied.

The kid at the front desk looked up at me briefly and then back down at his phone continuing to rapid-fire text. "Why are you telling me? You should have delivered it right to her apartment,"

"Sorry, but they forgot to include the unit number on the address."

Lie number two, Jayne you are going straight to Hell, do not pass go.

He heaved a sigh as if I was asking to bear his future children. Clicking on the keyboard with the same speed he said, "Unit six A. It's right around the corner in the first building on the left." He pointed in the general direction I needed to go and resumed his texting.

Checking the card, I saw the unit number for the recipient, Mrs. Jackson and dropped off her birthday bouquet, leaving her delighted and crying. Not quite as good as a real visit from her son, but at least he remembered her special day.

Sneaking back to unit six A, I rapped loudly on Evangeline's door. I could hear the loud squawking of a bird yelling, "Go away! Go away!" Heavy footsteps then shuffled slowly to the door. With only seconds before I expected the door to open, my stomach flipped like pancakes in an all-night diner, and I considered making a hasty exit. Too late. I watched the doorknob turn. It was go time, and I crossed my fingers hoping for questions to make their way from my brain to my tongue.

"May I help you?" an elderly overweight woman asked.

"I'm here to see Evangeline McArthur," I said trying to look into the apartment behind her, thinking this lady must be her mother, or maybe even her sweet old grandmother.

"Yes, that's me," she said.

An involuntary gasp escaped my lips. Franklin had definitely carved a path of destruction in her life. Where was the beautiful ingénue who had once been Evangeline?

"I know I'm not what people expect these days," she said with a forlorn half smile on her face.

I didn't know what to say to cover my obvious faux pas other than to charge forward with my false bravado.

"I... I'm Jayne Stanford," I said holding out my trembling hand, trying to cover my stammering.

"Oh yes. I should have recognized you immediately from your mug shot in the paper." She hesitated for a moment, and finally took my hand. "Please come in. I guess you're here to help me celebrate the death of the devil," she added.

The apartment opened up to a small living room with well-worn furniture and a few genuine antiques scattered about. On the far wall, occupying a pedestal, roosted her cockatoo, who still screamed at me to go away.

"I'm sorry for your loss?" It came out as more of a question than a statement. I took a few tentative steps into the room.

"I wouldn't even pretend to grieve over that pig. In fact, I opened my last bottle of champagne to celebrate."

I wondered if she bubbled over with enough anger to commit murder. I couldn't help myself so I just blurted out whatever rolled off my tongue.

"Did you hate him enough to kill him?" I asked.

She hesitated for only the blink of an eye before answering, "Yes, I did, and I hope he rots in Hell."

Berating myself for not having a way to record the

conversation, I racked my brain for a way to get more information from her. "Are you the one who stabbed him?"

"Foolish girl. I didn't kill him. I just said I was glad he was dead. If the police thought I did it why didn't they question me? You're the one who wound up in jail." She pointed her chubby finger in my direction, and suddenly didn't seem as grandmotherly as I originally thought.

"The police haven't spoken to you at all?" I asked in amazement.

They must be certain they had their "man" if they weren't even talking to other possible suspects. Despite the coolness of the apartment, I began to sweat.

I couldn't really imagine Evangeline being able to overpower the mayor. The life seemed to have been sucked out of her, leaving nothing left but a sad woman living alone with a mean bird.

"No one has contacted me," she said indignantly. "Is that why you came here, to accuse me?"

"I found your emails to him on a flash drive. He must have kept them for a reason," I said.

"So you know then, that he still owed me a hefty sum of money embezzled from my family. But that's not a secret, the entire state of Arizona knows."

"So if you didn't do it, and I didn't do it, who do you think might have wanted him dead?" I asked.

"That scumbag had more enemies than friends. He would have screwed over his own mother if she had something he wanted. Did you talk to his business associates, the Town Council members, the various girlfriends, or even the housekeeper?" She plopped her weight down in a chair that nearly groaned under her.

"Go away!" screamed the bird.

I shifted my weight from foot to foot, not sure if I should leave as the bird demanded, or sit down. Since she had not asked me to do either, I remained standing within reach of the door. Evangeline sat with her arms crossed over her ample bosom, staring at me, obviously willing to wait me out.

"I guess quite a few people wouldn't mind that the mayor is dead. I do wonder though, who stands to gain the most," I said.

"I'm just glad he can't suck any more money out of me. As you can see, there isn't much left." She waved her hand to demonstrate her meager existence. She seemed lost in thought for a moment, then stood. "Now, if you will excuse me, I have things to do."

I started out the door, my mind on overdrive, but remembered one last question I needed to ask her.

I turned just as she started to shut the door. "By the way, where were you on Friday night?"

After a long pause, during which she looked down at

the floor, she answered. "Life hasn't been easy since I met that jerk. I wish my addiction to him was as far as it went. You figure it out from there." She slammed the door in my face.

I vowed to do just that. She admitted to being enraged enough to kill him, and was delighted he was dead. I must be careful. If she was the true killer I could wind up as the next victim.

CHAPTER TEN

I drifted back to my car, lost in thoughts about the other people Evangeline said might harbor a reason to murder Franklin. I had to come up with someone soon, otherwise it looked like I would be on trial for his murder myself. My gut told me the Hummer person was involved. If not the killer, he or she was at least tangled up in the barbed wire of the situation.

Evangeline told me to question the Town Council. I knew the mayor wasn't adverse to blackmail so it's possible one of them had cause to shut him down. This motivated me to stop by the mayor's office in the Town of Cave Creek. If I was lucky there might be a clue to help me narrow the list of suspects.

I drove to Cave Creek Road and, just after Hohokam

Place, turned into the parking lot for the Cave Creek Town Council. The few cars in the parking lot gave me hope for quiet offices where I could glean some useful information from someone on his staff.

As I parked the car, a Maricopa Sheriff's Department vehicle pulled into the spot next to mine. I looked over at the deputy behind the wheel, and he looked at me. I froze, watching him unbuckle his seat belt and step from the car. A large gun, baton, extra bullets, handcuffs, and heavy-duty flashlight weighted down his duty belt. My hands stayed locked on the steering wheel in a death grip, unable to move. Was he there to take me back to jail? I could already feel the handcuffs tighten around my wrists, and nearly threw the car in reverse to make a run for it, when he walked past. He gave me a questioning glance and headed into the Maricopa County Sheriff's Department satellite office. I involuntarily shuddered at the reminder of my short-lived incarceration, and voiced a quick scornful laugh at myself for forgetting the two offices shared a parking lot.

I took a deep breath and squared my shoulders. Time to get some answers, instead of more questions. I headed into the Town Council offices.

"May I help you?" A woman of about my age sat behind the reception desk, her dull brown hair hung limply, brushing against the collar of her buttoned-up gray blouse.

She pushed up the over-sized glasses sliding down her nose.

I felt much like Bugsy must have when he caught a mouse and toyed with it. A pinch of guilt tugged at me, but I squashed it in the name of my mission.

I paused for a moment while my brain tried to come up with a plausible excuse. "I wanted to meet with the mayor about... ah, um... a personal matter."

She looked around. "The mayor passed away a few days ago." She whispered the words, and burst into tears. "He was a good man and he tried to do the right thing by this town."

"Oh my." Her reaction momentarily took me aback. Regaining my composure and focusing on my mission, I put my hand to my mouth and called on my best acting skills. "He was supposed to leave me an important personal document. Perhaps you have seen something with my name on it... Bailey Chauncey." Sorry, Bailey, I thought to myself since hers was the first name that popped into my head. Lie number three rolled off my tongue way too easily.

"He might have left something on his desk. I haven't been able to bring myself to go into his office since I heard the news. I'll just be a minute." She stood, sniffling into a tissue, and started toward his office, her shoulders hunched. I couldn't help but notice her long skirt and sensible, black, low-heeled shoes my grandmother surely would have admired. I followed before she could think of a reason to stop me.

The mayor's office looked the same as my apartment after its ransacking.

"What happened here?" She looked around in dismay. "It will take me hours to clean up this mess. I should probably go next door and report this to the Sheriff's Office."

"Maybe I could help you straighten things up and we'll find what the mayor left for me in the process." The last thing I wanted was a deputy hanging around.

"I guess that would be okay, but then I have to let the police know in case something important is missing. There is no council meeting today so I'm the only one here. I can't be away from the front desk for long." She glanced at me out of the corner of her eyes and I worried for a moment she, too, recognized my mug shot from the local news.

Together, we started picking up file folders while I made small talk to bond with her.

"Have you worked for the mayor long?"

Her voice so soft I had to strain to hear, she responded, "I worked for his predecessor and when Franklin, I mean Mayor McArthur, was elected he kept me on."

"I'll bet he couldn't have done the job without you."

She blushed. "He had a lot of good ideas for ways to improve the town. No one appreciated his genius."

I nodded as if I agreed with her assessment. "You must have known him when he was married to his wife."

"She isn't a very nice person. She didn't understand his vision."

I surreptitiously tried to look through as many of the files as I could to find any clues. Think Jayne, think. I closed my eyes and tried to put myself in the mayor's warped head, which was like trying to ride a wild Mustang—dangerous and frightening. If I were a criminal posing as a mayor, embezzling from charitable foundations and possibly blackmailing any number of people, where would I stash the evidence? Images of the mayor flipped through my head like a photo album. Except for the night of the murder, my only exposure with him was at the restaurant. Had he ever said anything that might help me find his killer? I remembered what he ordered, what he wore, and who he was with, but nothing he said stood out.

The phone started ringing and my new friend jumped up from her spot on the floor as if hit by an electric current. "I have to answer that." She looked torn between leaving me alone and doing her job as the lone town employee. "Are you okay here for a minute?"

"Sure, I'll just keep looking for my envelope."

"Okay but please don't touch anything else. My name is Sheila. I'll hurry right back." She dashed down the hall to answer the phone, her shoes squeaking with every step.

Seizing my opportunity, I quickly rummaged through the desk drawers, but found nothing significant. The stack of files all seemed to relate to town business. Something here *must* point in the direction of a potential killer.

I could hear Sheila's voice on the phone winding down the conversation, and knew my time was up. I hurriedly grabbed his monthly planner and stuffed it in my purse. I started for the door, and ran headlong into Trent Hayworth, with Sheila nipping at his heels.

"Don't I know you from somewhere?" he asked, leaning closer to examine me.

"No, I don't think we've met." I ducked my head, and tried to move around him.

"Franklin was reviewing some Foundation files and I need them for the auditors," he said to Sheila as he looked around the office.

He was selling, but I wasn't buying. His hands twitched and I was pretty sure he wanted to do his own search for incriminating materials. My mind replayed that fateful night at the cocktail party when the mayor demanded his share of the take. What had he said? If only my mind would stop spinning like a carnival ride, it might come back to me. The harder I tried to remember, the more difficult it became.

"Aren't you in charge of the women's shelter? How is that coming along?" I asked knowing that would provoke him.

"Yes, I am and it's right on schedule. We just need to wrap up a few more permits the mayor was handling, and we should be able to start construction." He was a much better liar than me, but I knew the truth.

I decided to go in for the kill and see what kind of reaction I would get. "Funny, I heard the construction was stalled due to funding."

"I beg your pardon?" Trent looked uneasily from Sheila to me.

"Sheila, would you mind giving us just a minute?" I pushed her toward the office door and closed it in her face despite her whimpering objections. I turned to Trent. "I don't have time to tip-toe around you, so I'm going to get right to the point. I'm tired of defending myself, and I need to get my life back. I know the mayor was blackmailing you. Did you kill him?"

"I do know you! You're that clumsy girl from the mayor's cocktail party. How dare you accuse me! You don't have any proof... do you?" Trent started out roaring, but ended his sentence like a lamb.

"Not yet, but I'm working on it."

Trent stepped so close I could smell his perspiration

and the garlic he had at lunch on my face. "You better be careful if you know what's good for you. Maybe I did kill him and perhaps I'll finish the job with you."

I leaned back against the walnut desk in an effort to regain my composure and put some space between us. "I heard you argue with him the night he was killed," I sputtered, all courage abandoned.

Trent gave a sinister chuckle. "You don't have any proof that anything was happening between him and me, or you wouldn't be digging around in his office. Besides I have an airtight alibi. I went directly home after the party and was up early coaching my son's softball game. I have at least fifty witnesses."

"You're here for a reason," I said skirting around the desk and picking up a stack of files. You think he left something here that could incriminate you. If it's here I will find it."

Trent followed close behind me and reached to pull the folders from my hands. We struggled and the folders flew in the air, showering pieces of paper down all around us. In a frenzy, we both dropped to our hands and knees, and fought to grab whatever we could reach, only managing to tear papers from each other's hands.

Hearing the commotion, mousey Sheila found her inner lioness and burst back into the room. "You both have to stop. You're violating his memory!" Sheila howled as we rolled around on the floor. "I'm calling the police." Only, she didn't move.

Yanking the last page from my hands, Trent stood and rushed out the door, almost knocking her over in his haste. I remained on the floor, surveying the mess we made and wondering if I managed to snatch anything of importance. My gaze caught a small model airplane sitting on the shelf opposite the mayor's desk with a familiar symbol painted on the side.

Sheila scurried back to the desk, wringing her hands.

I stood, leaving the mess of papers strewn over the floor, and wondering how I would make my own quick exit.

"I'm going to get into trouble for this mess," she whined.

I really wanted to make a run for the door, but she looked so sad and lost I couldn't help myself. "I'm sorry. I don't know what came over me. I'll stay and help you put things in order. If you find something missing when we're done, you can walk over to the sheriff's office and report it."

She dabbed at the tears welling up in her eyes. "No, it's probably better you leave, and if I find anything with your name I will call you."

I didn't want to push my luck any further, and another confrontation with the police wasn't in my best interest, especially not in the office of my supposed victim. Disappointed I accomplished nothing at the mayor's office, I picked up my purse to leave. On impulse, while Sheila's back was turned, I grabbed the model airplane and hurried out.

I putt-putted on home to my empty apartment. I found no humor in driving the clown car and no joy in going home without Bugsy there. I checked my cell phone, seeing only a missed call from Bailey. No call reporting my cat had been found. No word from my attorney saying the murder charge had been dropped. No call from Jonas telling me he couldn't live without me.

As I opened my front door, I saw an envelope apparently slid underneath while I was away. I swallowed the lump in my throat. Was this more bad news? Couldn't be an eviction notice because my rent wasn't yet due. I ripped open the envelope to find a copy of my missing cat flyer with a bold red slash through his face. I gasped and dropped the note. Written below his photo someone printed a warning, "Return what you have of mine or else."

Maybe my kitty was alive and being held for ransom. I should have been disturbed or outraged, but instead I felt hope. Even if this wasn't proof, my gut told me Bugsy was alive! I didn't care about my job, my bills or even the possibility of a life behind bars. Well, life behind bars still posed a major concern. Still, I had something to hold on to, even if only a small chance I could save him. "Momma is coming, Bugsy, hang on." I sang out to the walls. This is one thing I would do. I could do. The only questions were how, and what the heck did I have that belonged to someone else?

I needed to focus. To do that, I needed a serious infusion of chocolate. I sat on the kitchen counter and ate the sole cupcake that survived the assault. I expected a long night ahead, so I washed it down with a few of the Diet Mountain Dews.

I powered up my computer and checked my email to see if Bailey sent me anything else from mayor McArthur's flash drive. Is it possible there might be something I had overlooked? I licked the chocolate off my fingers and clicked through the emails. Evangeline really despised Franklin, but her main focus was to emancipate her family's money from Franklin's stash. She lived a meager existence with her nasty bird and I could understand wanting to get back what he stole from her. My gut told me she wasn't involved.

Changing my tactic, I decided to look through the monthly planner I nabbed from the office to see who he might have met with recently. Maybe it would give me some clues as to anyone else with a reason to want him dead. Although Trent was looking like the most likely candidate, especially after he threatened me earlier, it was unlikely he would have slipped back to the mayor's house that night. I had seen no cars on the road until Jonas came along. He made a point of telling me he was occupied early in the morning, so maybe before coaching his son's game he decided to shut the mayor up once and for all.

The planner showed appointments with council members, public hearings, lunch and dinner dates with different people, none of whom were familiar to me. I couldn't find a pattern or anything that looked suspicious. I was frustrated and just about to give up for the rest of the day when my phone started barking. I knew without glancing at the Caller ID it was Bailey as she had programmed her own ringtone into my phone.

"You won't believe the day I've had," I said without even a hello.

"You won't believe the day I've had either. I broke into the encrypted files on the flash drive and it's full of pornographic pictures."

"So the sleazy mayor downloaded porn. Somehow that doesn't surprise me."

"This isn't just any old porn. These are pictures of someone you know with a young boy and a woman. At least I think it's an underage boy, but I'm not sure. I'm shocked, but I'm not shocked. Do you know what I mean? " Bailey was excited by this discovery, and I had to wait for her to take a breath to jump in.

"Who?"

"Trent Hayworth!"

"Holy cow. He's a married man with kids. That's what the mayor must have had on him."

Bailey took a deep breath and I prepared myself for another rapid-fire round.

"It's always a good idea to encrypt files when you want to keep sensitive information from falling into the wrong hands. Not such a good idea to use a simple password philosophy to open them. I started with my usual process when I'm working with a client to see how protected their data really is. Generally, and in this case it was true as well, the protections in place aren't up to par. I would have broken into the files sooner but I got sidetracked by an urgent request from my German client," she announced triumphantly.

"So Franklin McArthur somehow got pictures of Trent in a compromising situation and was blackmailing him. That we know. Now we need to figure out how he got them, who else is in them and if he was blackmailing others."

"Have you found anything else?" Bailey asked.

"I just came from his office in town and got my hands on his planner, but so far that's given me zilch. Wait, there was a key in my apron pocket. Hold on, let me find it. I know I stuck it somewhere in the kitchen but that was before the apartment was ransacked. Now I can't find anything."

"Your apartment was ransacked? What are you talking about?"

"Ah, I didn't want you to freak out but someone broke in last night and trashed my apartment. I don't care about the break-in because there's nothing here to steal apparently." I choked up thinking about Bugsy. I wanted to tell Bailey about the note, but I was starting to worry that I could put her in danger. I hate keeping secrets, and it goes against my nature to lie—most of the time—but I bit my tongue and glossed over it.

I paused for only a heartbeat to gather my wits. "It was probably just kids. I called the police, and since there wasn't forced entry, it looks like I must have left the back patio door unlocked and someone just threw stuff around. Probably some teenagers with nothing else to do. Maybe they thought it was funny."

"That's not funny. Did it happen while you were at work?"

I paused again, remembering that Bailey didn't know about the layoff. If I told her I was out of work she would insist on giving me money, and I couldn't let her do that after she already posted my bail. I compromised with myself by deciding to tell part of the truth and just leave a few facts out.

"Yeah, after I left for work. I'll just put things back in

order, but you probably wouldn't notice much difference in the before break-in versus after." I forced a laugh to try to get her mind off the seriousness of the situation.

"Maybe you and Bugsy should stay with me for a few days."

"No, that isn't necessary. I need to do a good cleaning around here anyways," I said hurriedly as I dug around in the kitchen looking for the key. "Can you email me those pictures and I'll see if I recognize anyone besides Trent."

I didn't relish looking at Trent Hayworth naked, in fact it made me more than a little nauseous, but I had to follow up on every lead. After a few more minutes of convincing Bailey that I would be fine in the apartment and letting her think I had to get ready for work, we hung up.

With nothing else to do at the moment, I decided it was time to straighten things up. I taped the note about Bugsy on the refrigerator and slogged through the kitchen first. I knew I had placed the key someplace safe but, with my little home in shambles, it was hard to find anything.

It took me an hour to put the kitchen back in order, and I didn't find the key. Next I tackled the small living room, and then my bedroom. Three hours later, I had a cleaner apartment than before the mystery intruder had ravaged it. Replenishing my caffeine supply with another Diet Mountain Dew I looked around and tried to remember my thought process of three days ago. My life had become one wild barrel race against time, and if I didn't stop and catch my breath I suspected it would only get worse.

Evening was coming on, so I thought I would open my emails to look at the photos Bailey would have sent by now. I downloaded twelve emails from her, all with attachments. Steeling myself, I opened the first one and looked at the photo. There was no doubt it was Trent kissing a young man.

Having worked in the restaurant for a while I was getting better at judging ages. Invariably, an underage person would come in and try to order a drink. Some people would always look older than their real age, but the few lucky ones would appear younger. In my head, I would always be younger than my real age, but looking in the mirror was a constant reminder that the years were creeping up on me. I could tell the young man in the photo was definitely over eighteen even though he was dressed like a high school wannabe rapper. Trying to find a positive in the situation, I thought even if Trent was a murderer he wasn't involved in child pornography.

The next few photos showed the two men in progressive states of undress. Opening the fifth photo I stopped. I knew this person. I had seen her in the restaurant. This was the woman who came in and sat at the end of the bar to meet her dates. Naïve me thought she was on an Internet dating service, but Emmett had sworn otherwise. I couldn't help but be mesmerized by the image.

I clicked to the next photo and she was partially undressed. Wearing boy shorts and a skimpy bustier, she held a whip. Trent was fully undressed and splayed out on the bed with one hand tied to the bedpost. Something about the picture wasn't right. Trent's eyes were closed and his head lolled over to the side. Even though it had been awhile since I had been naked with a man, this didn't look like someone in the throes of passion. More like someone who had imbibed one too many shots of tequila, or maybe even been drugged.

I clicked through a few more pictures with the other two in various stages of undress around Trent. I assumed that the mayor took the pictures, but that didn't make any sense to me. How would he have convinced Trent to allow him to take the pictures if Trent had been conscious? I clicked back through all the photos taking a longer look at each one. On the eleventh photo, something caught my eye that I had missed in the first run-through. In a partial reflection from the mirror, I made out a blurry image of a woman's hand wearing a large ring with diamonds in the shape of an S. My old monitor wouldn't show a clear image when I zoomed the photo in closer. I held no doubt in my mind that a woman took the pictures, and she was probably the director of the entire scene as well. My brain tried to make the connection between Trent and Evangeline. If the rumors had been true about drug abuse, then perhaps she helped drug Trent, and was the one taking the pictures. But how would Franklin have gotten them from her? I was pretty sure she wouldn't be helping him, even if blackmail was one way to get back the money he owed her. Then again, anything was possible.

My head started to hurt from staring at the images. Unfortunately they were now burned indelibly into my brain. I could see them when I closed my eyes, and knew they would haunt my dreams when I finally called it quits and tried to sleep. I missed Bugsy, and I couldn't sleep fitfully until he was safely back at home snuggled in next to me, hogging most of the bed.

My head throbbed and my hair was a tangled mess from non-stop twirling around my fingers. This was way too much thinking for me to do after a day like today with only soda and a few cupcakes to keep me going. It was after nine o'clock, but I decided to order a pizza and continue plugging away.

Standing to stretch my back, I accidentally knocked over the mug I kept ink pens in, which Bailey had made me in her ceramic phase. I picked up the mug, grateful it hadn't broken. Fate was finally dealing me a better hand as, mixed in with the pens, I found the key.

I contemplated the number stamped on the side and the dangling pewter tag with a logo I didn't recognize. The logo appeared to be the letter V with a small arc down to the left, ending with an airplane. Looking over at my end table, there sat the model airplane I had removed from the mayor's office.

I twirled the pewter tag around my finger while staring at the model. I was sure there was a connection between the two. The model was of a small twin propeller plane, but the key had the letter V and didn't look like something that would start a plane. Despite myself, I chuckled because I wasn't even sure you used a key to start the engine of a plane. Guess I could Google it and find out. I started searching airplane names to try to find one that started with the letter V or something that had the Roman numeral for five. After fifteen minutes of finding nothing, the pizza arrived. I dug in my coffee can cuss penalty stash to pay and tip the delivery boy. He wasn't thrilled to be tipped in quarters, but my motto is it all spends the same.

Munching on a slice loaded with extra cheese and pepperoni, and I looked at the key again which had fallen to the floor in my haste to answer the door for dinner. From this angle it didn't look like a V at all, but rather an A with the slash and airplane moving up to the right. The slash represented the vapor trail left in the wake of the plane as it traveled across the sky. I recognized it now as the logo for the Scottsdale Air Center. My subconscious was working overtime and had connected the key to the plane without me realizing it. Finally, I may have found a purpose to use this weird memory.

Emmett and I worked a private party at the Air Center last year. I closed my eyes and massaged my scalp to get the blood flowing. Think, Jayne, think. We served jumbo shrimp wrapped in prosciutto, beef crostini with horseradish sauce, crab stuffed mushrooms and... Stop! I need to focus on the airpark and not the food.

I remembered driving up to the modern steel terminal with its floor-to-ceiling glass windows. Before you walked in the front doors, you could view the landing strip with planes parked on the tarmac in anticipation of the next luxurious trip. There were chauffeurs standing like sentries beside their long black limousines waiting to ferry passengers to some fabulous resort. The spacious lobby area held a receptionist and concierge ready to handle the passenger's any wish, from booking a suite at the Four Seasons to arranging tee times at one of the many top-rated golf courses. I wondered if they might perhaps book other types of gentleman's entertainment.

We set up in the Pilot's Lounge area furnished with comfy leather recliners spaced so no one invaded another's personal space while watching the forty-two inch plasma television mounted on the wall. At the time, I was most impressed by the hand-blown dishes of candy placed in several locations for the pilots to snack on while waiting for their flight time. Typical of me to remember something associated with chocolate.

I also recalled quiet rooms where the pilots could nap between flights, and even showers. But I couldn't recall seeing anything this key would fit.

Before I realized it, I had eaten half the pizza and the clock read well past two in the morning. I needed to get some sleep, vowing that tomorrow I would head over to the Air Center and try the key in every lock until I found what it fit. Between the flash drive and the key, the pieces were starting to fall into place. If I could gather enough evidence, I could go to the police and prove my innocence. I needed to put them all together in one big happy meal before time was up for either Bugsy or me.

CHAPTER ELEVEN

I didn't sleep well which may have been the result of eating so much pizza, drinking a six-pack of Diet Mountain Dew, or just my mental state. I tossed and turned in my bed, never able to get fully comfortable and block out the pictures of Trent. Despite that, I awoke by eight o'clock after only a few hours of sleep. I was anxious to drive down to Scottsdale to, hopefully, unlock a few of the mysteries surrounding the mayor before his death.

I knew I wouldn't be allowed beyond the reception desk if I didn't dress the part. For once, I wished I had some designer outfit salvaged from Goodwill. I dug around in my closet which, due to the break-in, was now quite well organized. It was an unwritten rule... if you wanted to hang out in Cave Creek you wore your Western gear. If you wanted to hang out in Scottsdale, even just to go shopping at the mall, you had to dress like a Scottsdale socialite.

I found a pair of jeans Bailey gave me for a birthday, embellished with beading down the legs. This clean closet was working out well for me, as I hadn't seen those jeans in months. I squished into them, mentally yelling at myself for eating pizza so late at night, and found a tank top to match. I layered on all the costume jewelry I owned to imitate affluence, and put on my highest heels. I felt like the world's tallest woman, but sometimes my height could work to my advantage. To finish the look, I used the hair dryer to blow out my natural curls.

Looking in the mirror, I decided the only thing missing was the attitude. Otherwise, I guessed I could pass for someone's bitchy girlfriend or maybe the wife of an important man. I grabbed the key and hit the road with a mission. I was not going to leave the Air Center until I found what the key fit. Maybe it would lead to nothing at all, but I didn't think it would have wound up in my apron if someone didn't want me to find the contents. Possibly, it was the quickest place to hide it but, either way, I had it now and planned to use it. Whether it was Franklin or someone else who put the key in my apron I wasn't sure, but my gut told me I now moved in the right direction.

The Air Center was just as I remembered it—all glass and steel. I parked on the street, not wanting to draw attention to my little rental car. Let the staff think I arrived in one of the limos waiting out front. Unfortunately, yet again, I hadn't formulated a plan beyond getting in the front door and asking someone to point me in the right direction.

I sashayed up to the receptionist with my head held high, "Excuse me, but my husband asked me to come down and pick up something for him. But silly me, I was so busy at Tiffany's I forgot to pay attention about where to go. Can you tell me what this key opens?"

The young woman behind the reception counter eyed me suspiciously, but took the key from my hand and looked up the number on her computer.

"This goes to locker 17 in Hanger Three," she said handing it back to me.

"Oh, perfect. I'll just go over there and get what he needs." I started toward the back doors leading to the tarmac.

"I'm sorry, ma'am, but you aren't allowed to go back there without the proper credentials."

"But I have his key," I said inching closer to the door.

Her eyes darted over to the corner where the security guard stood and gave a slight nod. "You could call your husband and ask him to bring his ID card and then we can let him go to the hanger, but I cannot let you beyond these doors."

My bravado faded fast as the security guard

approached.

It occurred to me that if the locker belonged to Franklin McArthur, she might put two and two together and come up with accused murderer.

"Very well. He'll be upset with me for not paying attention to him, but I'll go home and tell him he has to run his own errands." I started toward the front doors.

The security guard eyed me skeptically, but didn't make a move to follow me out the door, which I took as a good omen. However, here I was so close and still not able to get into the locker.

I sat in my car, tapping my fingers against the steering wheel. I had to find a way to get into that hanger. I wasn't ready to give up this easily, and I needed answers. I considered waiting around for the shift change and trying the routine again, but without an ID card I didn't expect to get any further than I did the first time.

Sometimes even a blind squirrel can find a nut, and I looked over to see the large iron gates opening to allow a maintenance vehicle out. I didn't think about what I was doing, I just reacted to the opportunity as it presented itself. As the maintenance truck pulled out, I hit the gas and squeezed through just before the gates closed.

Looking left and right, I tried to think logically about which way the hangers would be numbered. Guessing they would start at one end and go down the row, I counted from the side farthest from me. There were four hangers total, so Hanger Three would be the first one on my left. It looked like I could drive behind and park, possibly where I wouldn't be noticed immediately. I hit the gas again and cruised down to what I hoped was the right hanger.

On the far side of the buildings shone the black tarmac of the airstrip, heat radiating off it like a mirage. I could see the parked planes lined up like ladies waiting their turn for the stage in a beauty pageant. A few cars parked between the hangers, but I didn't see anyone milling around. I could only pray the vehicles belonged to pilots who were either relaxing in the lounge or out on a flight. I parked as close as I could to the entrance and slid out of the car, making sure to take the locker key with me and hide my purse under the seat. If anyone stopped me, I didn't want to have to show my driver's license. Best they didn't know my name.

I hurried around to the entrance and crossed my fingers, hoping I would not find the door locked. I preferred not to have to climb in a window, but if it came to that I would wait until dark and do it then. I grasped the doorknob and turned it slowly, giving a push as I did. It opened easily and my jaw dropped. The sight filled me with awe, like looking at the reflection of mountains on a crystal clear lake. Four private jets, each trying to outshine the others, stood in military precision with their noses pointing toward the large center bay doors.

The area yawned at least three times the size of a football field. It would take me an hour just to walk from one end to the other in these heels. So much for a quick in and out. I looked around the outside walls. The receptionist mentioned lockers, so there must be a central area for the pilots and passengers to congregate. I hoped it would be near the front and close to the parking lot. Just on the other side of the large hanger entrance, I saw a door but couldn't read the sign from where I stood. It meant walking in front of the open hanger doorway, but I had no other option.

I figured I might as well keep playing the role and act as if I belonged there. I prayed no one would be in the locker area. Marching as fast as I could in the heels with my head held high in as snobby a fashion as I could manage, I made it all the way to the door without seeing anyone.

I inhaled deeply, pushed open the heavy door and peered around. The room was a smaller version of the pilot's lounge in the terminal. There was a kitchenette, several cushiony chairs, a wide screen television and the apparently obligatory bowl of candy. Unable to resist, I grabbed a handful as I moved through the room. On the opposite side there were two doors labeled as women's and men's restrooms. I opted for the women's first, out of habit. Inside,

I found shower facilities, as well as a small lounge area for sleeping or freshening up. Several lockers lined the wall, but none of them were numbered seventeen. That left the men's locker room. *Please just get me through this one last thing and I swear I will be a much nicer person,* I prayed.

I crept out of the ladies' locker room and listened at the door of the men's, unwrapping a chocolate while I built up the nerve to walk in. The last time I ventured into a men's room I was seventeen at a rock concert. The line for the ladies' restroom was too long so, as did many other girls, I hit the men's room to speed up the process. This one had the same layout, only not quite as nice as the ladies' side. Moving more quickly after my infusion of chocolate, I found locker seventeen. I dug the key out of my pocket and slid it into the keyhole. I chewed my bottom lip. Who knew what might be in this locker? If this belonged to the mayor, anything was possible. The metal door opened with a creak and inside lay a plain black gym bag. I couldn't believe I had gone to this much trouble for his smelly, dirty gym clothes.

"Excuse me but I think you're in the wrong room!"

Startled out of my reverie, I pulled the bag out of the locker and gathered my courage before I turned and looked straight into the eyes of a wet naked man. As much as I knew I shouldn't do it, I couldn't prevent my eyes from darting down his body. They kept moving from his slack jowls to his hairy mammoth beer belly and down. Why did I have to look down? My brain registered a resounding *eew gross,* and mortification gushed from my pores.

"What do you think you're doing?" he asked again.

"Oops."

As I dashed for the door, I managed to add a feeble "I'm sorry" and never looked back. I threw the bag over my shoulder and started to run back across the polished hanger floor, slipping in the high heels. What was I thinking when I picked these shoes? Oh yes, I was thinking I would waltz in the door and they would hand me the keys to the terminal as if I were the Queen of Scottsdale.

As I sprinted across the open hanger doorway, I saw a distant pickup truck travelling quickly in my direction. It wasn't just any pickup. Lights flashed in the grill and across the top. The security forces were headed my way.

Tripping in my heels on the gravel, I ran back across the parking lot to my car. The keys were in my purse, which of course was successfully hidden under the seat. I scrambled to dig the purse out, and then the keys, which naturally fell to the bottom again. Finally, slamming the key in the ignition, and threw it in reverse. I had to make it to the exit before the forces arrived or got back-up from the real police. Even though it hadn't occurred to me when I started this mission, I was pretty sure breaking into an airport terminal would go against at least one federal law. Forget worrying about a murder rap, I would go down for a National Security violation.

Before I could get back on the road to the exit, the security patrol pulled up beside me. I could see the cords bulging in his neck and his mouth screwed up in a snarl. His face beet-red he pointed his finger at me. Decision time. I could stay here and play dumb or I could make a run for it. I picked choice two. I waited until he got out of the truck and was almost to my window before I hit the gas going backwards. The blood rushed through me as adrenaline took over. I became conscious of clenching the steering wheel and my whole body tensed. Once I was out of his reach, I threw the automatic transmission into low gear to grab more traction, punched the accelerator all the way to the floor, and slammed it back in drive. I swerved to the left and was now heading away from the direction I wanted to go. I was pretty sure the little car had never given more of itself before. The guard recovered from his shock blazingly fast and followed hot on my trail. Traveling at a speed that might just take us airborne, I swerved around a set of barricades, squealing the tires, but didn't dare slow down. The truck's security lights flashed in my side mirror and the guard came so close to my bumper I could clearly see his enraged face bellowing at me. I spun the wheel to the left and tried to aim my car back in the direction of the hangers.

The speedometer registered ninety and I was headed for a twelve-foot high chain link fence. As much as I had come to have faith in the little car, no way would we be able to bust through it to make it to Frank Lloyd Wright Boulevard. Even if I could, I would be crossing six lanes of traffic at a perpendicular angle, which didn't leave much chance of survival. I changed direction again at the last minute feeling more and more like a barrel racer in the world championships. Only, instead of a trophy, I would win my life.

The guard stayed hot on my tail, and I guessed he would have backup any second. I burned up the tarmac on a long straight stretch, finally heading in the right direction. For a flash, I diverted my gaze to the rearview mirror, surprised to find he wasn't on my tail anymore. When I looked forward again I locked wide eyes with a pilot headed directly for me trying to land. Holy cow, I was on the runway! I heard the screaming before I realized it was me. It was too late to hit the brakes, and there was nowhere to turn.

"I'm going to die!" I screamed.

I looked at the pilot and he looked at me, and I closed my eyes. Instinctively, I ducked down in the seat, but kept the pedal to the floor and hung on. I swore I felt the heat of the plane as it glided over the top of the car. I'm not sure if the tires scraped the roof because I was still screaming louder than the roar of the engines. It was only a few seconds, but seemed to last forever. I opened my eyes and took my foot off the gas, I was alive. At that moment, nothing else mattered. Even if I was arrested, I was alive and that meant I had another chance.

At the end of the runway, a turn off loomed, and when I hit it doing my own flying at 75 mph the car tilted onto two wheels. I made it this far and I wasn't about to stop now. Around the first hanger I saw an exit, and aimed in its direction. The gates started to slowly open, forcing me to let off the gas again. I slipped the rental through before they were fully open and slammed onto Hayden Road. No one was behind me, but on the off chance he had the time to get my license plates, I decided to get out of Scottsdale faster than a throw from a belligerent bucking bull.

I switched off Hayden Road and moved over to Pima, even though it ran a mile farther east than I needed to head. It was less traveled, and I felt a modicum of safety. I kept driving and kept repeating my new mantra, "I'm still alive." When I reached Cave Creek Road, instead of turning left, which would take me home, I turned right toward Bartlett Lake. I needed some time to clear my head before I went home. If the police were waiting for me, I needed an alibi, or at least, a good reason for what I had just done. Add to my growing list of infractions the lives I almost took in the runway stunt.

I pulled over once I passed the last of the housing developments, and turned off the ignition. Reality finally sunk in and I couldn't suppress my hysterical laughter. Who was I? The Jayne I thought I knew would never have done some of the things I did in the last few days. Breaking and entering a dead person's house, charged with murder, a night in jail, confronting a sad ex-wife, wrestling on the floor of the mayor's office with a potential suspect and, finally, the fiasco at the airport. All that for a stinky gym bag? What was I thinking? Easy answer, obviously I jumped in without thinking—again. When would I ever learn?

The gym bag had fallen from the passenger seat to the floor during the great escape. I struggled to lift it, noticing its heavy weight for the first time. Adrenaline kicked in while I was at the airport and I hadn't paid any attention, presuming it was stuffed with his gym shoes, socks, and any other smelly paraphernalia he used to work out.

I unzipped the bag and gasped. Rather than workout gear, I discovered plastic bags filled with one hundred dollar bills. I pulled the first baggie out and stared at it for minutes, turning it over and over in my hand. All this money would resolve the financial problems I had, so why did I feel sick to my stomach? My heart told me what my head refused to admit. This money was dirty from the suffering of others. It definitely tied into the murder. The dilemma was what to do with it. I couldn't give it to the police, who may already be looking for me. This would only add motive for the murder. I couldn't take it home, since my apartment had been broken into once. I didn't want to involve Bailey, Emmett, or Jonas and possibly put them at risk, or even make them accessories to my crime spree.

My only other safe place was Wild Bronco. I had a small locker there to store my purse during my shift. I dug back into the gym bag to see if there was anything besides cash inside. Baggie after baggie was stuffed with more of the same one hundred dollar bills. I checked the side pockets and found a printed page with a list of names. Names I recognized as prominent business people, local and state politicians, a judge, and even a top-ranking police officer. I wondered if these were people who the mayor scammed for this money, or if they were somehow involved in stealing from others. Were they innocent victims or co-conspirators?

My curiosity got the best of me, and I knew I couldn't stash the cash without knowing how much I had. I counted the number of baggies and compared the sizes. They all appeared to contain the same number of bills, so I figured I could count one and multiply it by the number of baggies. I opened the first one, fanned the bills out across my lap and started counting. Fifty one hundred dollar bills later, my fingers cramped from counting. Five thousand dollars in each baggie, and I counted twenty baggies. One hundred thousand dollars in a smelly gym bag.

Bad Jayne popped up again and suggested I borrow a few of the bills to help me get by until I could work again. Rent was coming due and I needed money. As soon as I could work a few shifts, I would be able to pay the money back. I dug around the car, found a scrap of paper, wrote an I.O.U for $500, and stuck it in the baggie. On second thought, I scratched out the $500 and put $1,000. Just in case my leave was longer than I expected, this would carry me.

The next dilemma was if Peter would let me in the restaurant after he gave me this extended vacation. If I waited until the dinner rush was in full swing, I could possibly slip in the back and Peter wouldn't know I was there. The kitchen staff may wonder why I was bringing in a gym bag to leave in my locker. They all knew I hadn't seen the inside of a gym since high school, and what reason would I have to put my gym clothes in my work locker when I wasn't even supposed to be there? A better plan would be to find an excuse to stop by the restaurant and, when they were all distracted, sneak the bag into my locker. It may seem odd, but the easiest way to distract restaurant workers—and by far the best way into their hearts—was food.

Finally, the neurons began firing in my brain and I knew what I could do. It was already almost two o'clock in the afternoon. I had the cash to buy ingredients and I would bake a cake. Or, maybe I would just go to the gourmet market and buy a really good cake and put it on my plate. Something I knew my co-workers wouldn't be afraid to eat. I could say I had time on my hands so I wanted to do something nice like baking them a cake. While the chef cut the cake and the staff gobbled it up, I would stuff the bag in my locker.

It was time to get moving and put my plan in affect. I stopped by the market and picked up a chocolate cake that didn't look too perfect and headed home to my apartment. I drove around the development one time before I parked, just in case anyone was waiting to arrest me for the airport blunder. The coast was clear, so I parked in my spot and hurried in the house with cake in hand. I dug through my kitchen cabinets looking for a decent plate to slide the cake onto. By the time I got the cake off the cardboard and onto my plate it really did look like I could have baked it. The top layer had slid over and the entire cake leaned to one side. Add the thumbprint on the side, where I caught it before it started heading for the floor, and it was believable.

While home, I decided to switch the cash into a bag that looked more like something I would carry. I owned a large purse I called my "movie bag." Its size allowed me to bring my own candy and a super-sized water bottle. Then I would simply buy popcorn. It's not that I liked bringing my own candy, but I was always stretching my dollars. At the drug store, I could get three boxes of candy for three dollars instead of one box for three dollars at the movies. To be honest, I also liked mixing my different candies into one delicious bag so each bite was a surprise.

I stuffed the baggies of cash in the movie bag, and topped it off with a t-shirt I grabbed from the "still dirty, I need to do laundry" pile so it wouldn't be obvious to anyone if they happened to glance at the bag. With my disguised cash bag and cake in tow, I headed into Cave Creek and Wild Bronco. I would sashay in just in time for pre-shift but, with the cake in my hands, no one would care. As bizarre as this day had been, I truly felt I was making progress. All that insanity hadn't been for a bag of stinky gym clothes but, instead, actual clues! I didn't know what to do with the money and the list, but I wouldn't give up until I did.

CHAPTER TWELVE

I drove into Cave Creek with my money/movie bag and the cake, trying to hold onto it with my right hand so it didn't fly off the passenger seat. Knowing I had someone else's ninety-nine thousand dollars riding shotgun with me was enough to make me a nervous wreck, so I didn't need to add professional car cleaner to my resume. As fun as the clown car was to drive around, I would be happy when my old car Betsy was fixed and ready to drive again. That reminded me I should call Jonas and get an update on the car. I'd been so busy lately I hardly had time to think of anyone or anything, other than the current moment's calamity. Part of me had been hoping Jonas would call me, but at least the car gave me an excuse to talk to him.

Arriving at Wild Bronco, I pulled around back to the

employee parking. Even though I was on a forced vacation, Peter hadn't fired me. As I walked in the back door, balancing the cake and bag, I realized how much this place had become my second home. I needed to be at work, serving my regulars and doing what I seemed to do best.

The kitchen staff was in full swing prepping for the evening's meals.

"Hola, te he traído un regalo," I called out holding the cake for all to see.

"Hola, amor," called out Sal. "A gift for us? You made us a cake?"

"Si. Doesn't it look beautiful?"

Sal eyed the cake suspiciously. "Are you sure you made this? And if you did, are you sure it's edible?"

"Okay, so maybe I didn't make the cake, but it is on my plate and I know it's edible." I laughed unable to lie to him.

"What is the occasion?"

"I didn't have anything to do, so I thought I'd give you a well- deserved treat."

"We don't care what the reason is, we like cake!" Emmett walked up behind me and wrapped his arms around me. "How are you holding up?"

I wanted to tell Emmett the truth, but to tell him I had a bag of money so I was doing pretty well at the moment probably wasn't the best plan. I reasoned it was smarter to keep this secret to myself. "I'm doing okay. I miss you guys and I still haven't figured out who killed the mayor, but I think I'm making some progress."

"Be careful Jayney and don't get yourself killed in the process. Of course, if you do and Jonas is broken hearted, I would be happy to console him for you," Emmett said, giving me a nudge with his elbow.

"Hey now, buddy. First of all Jonas may have a little to say about that and, secondly, I don't plan on getting killed."

"Seriously, why don't you let the police do their job?"

"The police think the case is solved. Murder suspect, namely little old me, arrested. Now, all that's left is the trial. I can't wait around and hope that somebody figures it out before I'm hauled away."

"Just be careful and stay safe. It's really boring around here already, and we all miss you."

Peter marched into the kitchen "What's going on? We have to get the dining room set up before guests start arriving."

I couldn't resist getting a jab in. "Sorry, it's my fault. I had some free time on my hands and thought the crew could use a little treat before their shift starts." Looking at Emmett I added, "I guess not everyone has missed me."

Peter stood eyeing me with his hands on his hips. "Jayne, you shouldn't be here when you're not working."

If it had been a regular night at work, I probably would have given some quick comeback. This wasn't a regular night, though, and I desperately needed to get the bag of money into my locker before he threw me out.

I finished slicing the cake and made sure everyone had a piece. "I'll just put the plate in my locker." Looking around I added, "Because I have somewhere to go and I'm afraid it might break in the car." Not a realistic excuse, but it was the best I could come up with at the moment.

Peter stood with his head tilted to the side, pondering what I was up to.

"I guess it's okay, but these guys all have to get back to work." He turned to walk to the front of the house.

I was unconsciously holding my breath for the few seconds it took him to make up his mind and walk through the swinging door. The chefs all moved back to their prep stations, so only Emmett and I remained.

Walking with me to the women's small closet-sized locker area, Emmett draped his arm over my shoulders and leaned in close to my ear.

"So, spill it. Why are you really here?"

"I-I brought you cake," I said waving the now empty plate in his face.

"Yeah, and it was delish. But something's going on with you and you need to spill it right now."

"Okay, the truth is that I'm broke and I had to borrow money to get by. My apartment was broken into and my kitty is missing. Is that enough bad stuff for you?" I was starting to get myself worked up. "Oh yeah, and let's not forget I've been charged with murdering that schmuck of a mayor, and not only did I have to spend a night in jail I could be there for the rest of my life if the real killer isn't found."

Emmett wrapped his arms around me and gave me a huge, much needed hug. "I'm sorry, sweetie. It's all going to work out. You know I'm here for you."

"I know, and I love you for it, but I have to get through this on my own. It's enough to know I still have you in my corner." I hugged him tightly, choking back a sob.

"Emmett! Is your station ready?" Peter clamored from the dining room.

"I've got to go, but call me and keep me posted." Emmett gave me a hasty kiss on the cheek.

I opened my small locker. Having not been here for a few days, it was like seeing it for the first time. A large part of my current life was spent in the restaurant, and stuffed into this small metal box was its reflection. Pictures of Bugsy were taped to the door, as well as shots of Bailey and Emmett. Half a dozen hair scrunchies, a torn and stained apron, ink pens, a pair of socks—which were probably dirty—and a strange assortment of odds and ends thrown in at the completion of shifts. It almost made me sad that this was my life. *Get a grip, Jayne,* I told myself.

I stuffed the bag into the locker with great effort, balanced the plate precariously on the top, and slammed the door. If anyone knew I had the money, I couldn't imagine they would think I would stash it here. I waved to the guys in the kitchen and was almost to my car when I heard Emmett yelling behind me.

"Wait, I almost forgot. Someone called here and left you a message." He handed me a small pink slip of paper. "Don't forget to call me soon and let me know how you're doing." He said running back into the restaurant.

I unfolded the message and tried to decipher Peter's chicken scratch. He must have been livid to have to take a message as if he worked for me, instead of the other way around. I could picture his face getting red and imagine him spitting expletives while he wrote it. But he was just the kind of person who would make sure I got it, rather than toss it in the trash. I had to like that about him.

It looked like someone named Ricky had called and wanted to meet with me. I didn't know a Ricky, but I figured I should call the number and see what it was about. Maybe this person knew something about where Bugsy was. I realized that made no sense whatsoever, because how would a "catnapper" know I worked at Wild Bronco.

I dialed the number while sitting in my car.

"Who wants me?" A familiar voice asked.

"Ah, this is Jayne Stanford. May I speak to Ricky?"

A deep-throated chuckle preceded the response. "Miss Jayne, it's me Kiki. I have some information for you."

"Kiki from jail? How did you find me?" I was too stunned to wonder what information she could possibly have for me.

"Girl, I never forget anything someone says to me in jail. You never know when it will come in handy."

My brain was having a hard time following her. "So, Kiki, I guess you got bailed out of jail, too."

"Oh yeah, right after you did. Anyway, I have some information for you that I think may help you get out of that murder rap."

That got my full attention. "That would be fantastic! What is it?"

Kiki's voice became soft, almost a whisper, and I had to strain to hear her. "I can't talk right now, and certainly not on the phone. Meet me at nine o'clock tonight in the parking garage at the Scottsdale Quarter shopping center. Come alone, and don't tell anyone you are meeting me. Absolutely no one!"

"Okay, I'll be there." I said but she had already hung up.

I didn't know what else I could accomplish today. I dreaded going home without Bugsy there. My apartment seemed empty without my little ball of fur there to give me orders.

At least I now had some cash, so I could stop off at the store and replenish my cupcake and Mountain Dew supply. Maybe I would even buy something healthy for a change, like a salad. I knew I couldn't exist forever on sugar and diet soda, which in itself seemed to be a contradiction. I pulled into the grocery store, deciding against the gourmet market since I didn't need to splurge in the extreme, and walked inside trying to figure out what I should buy different from my usual.

An hour later, with bags full of healthy food and the usual fare of junk food, I was on my way home. I decided to make myself a well-deserved meal and then call Jonas. Since I had my nights free, maybe he would like to try that dinner thing again.

All the way home, I practiced what I would say to Jonas. A simple "I'm sorry I got arrested in the middle of our first date and would you like to try again," didn't seem like it would be enough to explain all the emotions churning around inside me. He was a good man, and part of me could see having a future with him. Another part reminded me of times when I jumped on the horse before making sure the cinch was tight. A guaranteed way to have a hard fall.

I feared making another huge mistake with my life and, if all of the emotional turmoil wasn't bad enough, who wants a serious relationship with a woman with her head on the block for a murder? I glanced at myself in the rearview mirror, it was impossible to miss the dark circles under my eyes, the lack of regular exercise and too many missed meals which all showed on my face. I looked like a waitress at the end of a twelve-hour shift at an all-night diner next to a college campus.

As I was trying to carry all eight bags of groceries up the sidewalk to my apartment, the figure of a man stepped out of the shadows. In my fright, I dropped the one bag containing my fruit supply for the week. Apples rolled one way and oranges took their own course down through the manicured lawn. I didn't know whether to run after the fruit or just run, in case this was the mysterious Hummer person.

"Hey, I didn't mean to scare you," Jonas said softly.

"You just about gave me a heart attack! What were you doing in the dark?"

"I stopped by the restaurant and your friend Emmett told me you were on extended leave," he said sadly.

"Oh, Jonas. My life is such a mess." I dropped the

rest of the bags and ran into his arms. All thoughts of protecting him from me followed my apples down the walkway out to the street.

Jonas wrapped his arms around me, resting his chin on the top of my head while he patted my back. My life was a complete wreck, but I hadn't felt this safe since the loss of my father. I was carrying around years of fear and insecurities like a worn-out teddy bear. I needed to trust this man and not be petrified my heart would get broken again.

Waves of relief washed through me and I felt like I could breathe. How long had I been holding my breath as if under water trying to break the surface, but hitting my head on a ceiling of ice, unable to swim to safety? I didn't need to swim by myself, I had Emmett to help pull me into the boat. I had Bailey to help me row to shore. And maybe I had Jonas, too. I wasn't all alone and I did have people who cared about me.

Jonas kept quiet for a minute, perhaps taken aback by my extreme reaction, for now I was sobbing into his shirt, unable to stop long enough to explain my epiphany. Just one big puddle of clinging woman.

"Come on now, darlin'. It's not that bad. We'll pick up your groceries," he said stroking my hair.

"I-I-I'm just so lucky to have you." I managed to get out between hiccupy sobs. "For a friend," I added in case he thought I was already planning the wedding.

"I won't argue that, but maybe we better take this in the house and let you catch your breath." He took my purse and dug out the front door key. Opening the door, he gently pushed me inside and went back out to retrieve my runaway groceries.

When he came back in with my oranges and apples all accounted for, he set the groceries on the counter, poured me a glass of water and brought it to me on the sofa.

"Stop, take a deep breath, and have a sip of water. Then we can talk." He looked around the room, "Is it cleaner than when I was here last? You must really have time on your hands."

I laughed despite myself. I'd forgotten how much happened that I never shared with Jonas. "A lot has been going on these last few days."

Jonas started putting my groceries away. He looked over his shoulder. "So why didn't you call me?" I could feel the temperature between us drop a few degrees.

"I don't want something bad to happen to you. I'm in this deep enough and you've already done so much for me."

"I'm a big boy, and I've been taking care of myself for a long time now."

"I know, but I'm going to see this through to the end and find out who really did kill mayor McArthur, and why that person is setting me up to take the fall." I stood and started to pace the room.

"Jayne, I don't think this is a job you should take on alone. Why can't you leave this to the police?" Jonas asked.

"I walked over to Jonas and, feeling brave, took his hand. "You are the best thing that has happened to me lately, and I may not have realized it before I saw you tonight. I really want us to get to know each other better, but first I have to do this for me. If we're going to have a chance, I need to get this behind me. Can you understand that?"

Jonas sat for a minute looking at our hands intertwined. "From the first time I met you walking in the dead of night, I knew you would be trouble. My head told me to watch out because you would take me for a wild ride. As fun as I knew that would be, I've already had my share of heartbreak, and don't want to fall for someone who would put me through it again."

I pretty much knew what he was going to say. I mentally tried to prepare myself for the big brush off. What sane man wants to get involved with a peculiar woman like me?

"It's okay, Jonas. I know what you're going to say," I interjected.

"Damn it, Jayne, give me a minute to finish. I have a million reasons why I should walk out that door and never look back. But I can't, because there is something about you I can't resist. Maybe it's because you make me laugh when no one else can. Maybe it's the way I can't stop thinking about you all day long. Maybe it's just the way you look in those jeans right now with your wild hair enjoying a life of its own. The way it makes me want to run my fingers through it whenever I'm near you. Or just maybe it's because you try so hard to be independent but I know you really need me more than I've ever felt needed. It makes me feel good."

I stood in stunned silence. I wish I had that darn voice recorder because that was one speech I would have liked to play back several times. Not being able to come up with anything as tender, or even clever, and knowing my mouth was probably hanging open anyways, I figured it was a good time for a kiss.

I can't ever remember a kiss that was sweeter or held more meaning than that kiss. Of course, the first kiss led to a few more, and some awfully wicked thoughts churned around in my head, but as much as I wanted to continue this in the bedroom, good sense finally prevailed.

"Jonas, I can't do this."

"Am I going to need to take a cold shower?"

"In the soap operas, when the building is burning down or the killer is just around the next corner, the hero and heroine have wild passionate sex."

"Huh?"

"Then somehow everything works out perfectly."

"I have no idea what you are talking about."

I sighed and tried again. "This is one of those times when, in a dream, you would pick me up and we'd roll around in the sheets and then—ta-da—there would be a happy ending. But in the real world, I'm facing a murder charge and I'm not ready to, you know."

I might have been tempted to rip his clothes off, but sensible Jayne reminded me my head was in enough turmoil without adding sex. Certainly not before I made sure I had on some new undies, and not before I laid off the cupcakes for a day or two.

"I don't understand half of what you said, but I get that you have a lot going on right now. We'll take it slow and see what happens."

I heaved a sigh of relief. "How about we dig through the groceries I brought and we'll rustle up some dinner?"

Before he could answer, I happened to glance over at the clock and realized it was five after eight. I was supposed to meet Kiki at nine o'clock. That left me just enough time to throw on some Scottsdale-appropriate clothes and rush down to our rendezvous. I couldn't tell him what I was doing since she had implicitly told me to come alone. If he knew, he might insist on coming with me as some sort of bodyguard.

My only choice was to hustle down and meet her, which meant I had to come up with an excuse to get Jonas out of the house.

"I just remembered I promised a friend I would run an errand for her. Can I have a rain check on dinner?"

Jonas looked at me curiously. "Sure." He stood up to leave, and I got the sense he felt like I was not being honest with him, which was true.

"We could meet up at One Eyed Jack's and grab a burger there if you want. This shouldn't take me long."

He considered it a minute, "It's getting late and I have to work early tomorrow."

I couldn't hide the disappointment on my face or in my voice, "I understand."

"How about we make it tomorrow night? I'll pick you up and we'll go early enough to catch some of the bull riding."

"Like a real date?"

He laughed. "Yes, a real date."

I walked him to the door and we shared another lingering kiss, which was almost enough to make me forget my troubles and my name.

"If you don't stop that, you won't run your errand and I won't be going home tonight," he said holding me at arm's length.

Fifty-seven seconds after his truck pulled out of my complex, I threw on a pair of super high stiletto heels, a short skirt and tight t-shirt, and headed out the door. I wanted to blend in with the Scottsdale crowd, and this was the only outfit I could find on short notice that would do the trick.

I had to stand on the gas pedal to get my little rental car to hurry along to Scottsdale. It could take twenty minutes, or forty, depending on the time of day, road construction, and traffic. Poor little clown car had really been put through its paces today. I promised to run it through the car wash tomorrow to ease my guilt.

I pulled into the first floor of the parking garage at eight fifty-five. I wasn't sure on what level to look for her, so decided to just keep driving around until I saw her. The shopping center was hopping with people, browsing the designer shops. In Scottsdale, there was always a new hip place to hang out, so the garage was almost full and I had seen people swarming the sidewalks when I arrived. No sign of Kiki on the first two levels, so I continued up until I was on the open-air top level. Only a few cars had bothered to park up this high, so I was just about to turn around and head back down when I spotted her getting out of a black Lincoln Navigator in the far corner.

She must have been waiting for me to arrive, as she frantically waved me over.

I pulled the rental car in next to her and got out. "Hey, Kiki," I said in greeting.

She looked around and peered into my car to see if anyone came with me. Without saying a word, she motioned for me to follow her. We walked to the corner overlooking the shops and restaurants below. She sat on the ledge, and suddenly I got a bad feeling about the situation. What could Kiki know about the mayor's murder? She drove a colossal tank of a car that could have replaced the huge black Hummer. How was Kiki involved? What it her plan was to get me here and kill me, too? I had to ask myself why I kept throwing my rope before I checked to see if the steer was a bull.

CHAPTER THIRTEEN

Why am I so stupid that I didn't tell Jonas where I was going? I felt my throat constrict and didn't know what to say, or if I should just run.

"Hey, kid, don't look so freaked out. I'm here to help you," Kiki said reading my mind, or maybe just observing my wide eyes and nervous fidgeting. "Nice outfit, got a hot date later on?"

I cut to the point, "Why did you ask me to meet you here?"

"Relax, enjoy the view of the beautiful people. Look at them all down there spending money they don't have on things they don't need. Too bad they can never fill up the holes in their lives."

I looked over the edge of the half wall at the busy

shoppers below. "I think I'll just stay here." I braced my hands on the wall and blurted out the question I wanted answered. "Kiki, do you know something about the mayor's murder?"

Kiki's laughter reverberated off the building across from us and several people actually glanced up. "That's what I like about you Jayne. You're a straight shooter." Realizing she was attracting unwanted attention, Kiki dropped her voice.

"My employer had some business with the mayor from time to time. I didn't connect the dots until yesterday. A while back, my boss asked me and one of the other escorts to do a job. Sometimes if the money is really good there might be some kinky stuff thrown in. I was told the guy wanted a three-way with bondage. Something about it didn't sound right and I passed, but I heard rumors."

"What did you hear?"

"This is only a rumor, and I won't testify to it, but I heard that the party planner was the mayor and he liked to encourage people to cooperate with him. He didn't mind getting creative, if you know what I mean."

I felt like an idiot, but I had to say, "No, I don't know what you mean."

Kiki stood on the half wall, walking along it as if on a gymnast's balance beam. Her bravery in her wedge sandals impressed me. "My boss told me the mayor liked to set up special parties, and stash away some evidence in case he ever needed it."

The pictures Bailey found confirmed this. "Kiki, did you ever go to these parties?"

"Now, now don't ask me to tell tales on myself. Girl, I wasn't born yesterday."

I tried a different tactic. "Do you know anyone who may have been at one of the mayor's parties? I found some pictures I think the mayor was using as blackmail. If it's true, it may lead to who killed him."

She balanced on one leg. "If you have pictures, you need to be careful. I could ask around, but I doubt anyone will talk to you. What did you do with the pictures?

She was making me nervous strutting back and forth on the ledge. "They're on a flash drive I kind of found. Kiki, you're scaring me. Maybe you should get down from there."

"Come on, Jayne, you only live once, you gotta take some chances every once in a while. Listen, my boss would pay good money for those pictures, but I'm going to tell you as a friend to steer clear of him. Two people who run this town when it comes to my business, and you don't want to mess with either of them."

I nodded in agreement.

She did a pirouette and walked back to me. "There's

something else you should know. I have a friend, Jimmy, who worked a few of the mayor's parties. Next thing I hear he's gone missing. At first I thought he skipped town with some of those pictures and some cash that disappeared at the same time. But yesterday I get a call from his mom saying she had to identify his body at the morgue."

"Oh no! What happened to him?"

"They said it was an overdose. I knew this kid, and he did have a problem, but he'd been clean for six months and was working the program. I know that for a fact because we were in NA together and I saw him there all the time. Funny, I even saw the mayor's ex-wife there a few times. Remember, you didn't hear any of this from me."

"Evangeline McArthur goes to NA?" I asked incredulously. I wondered if she had been at a meeting the night the mayor was murdered. I thought that should be relatively easy to verify. I could just go to the next meeting and see if she showed up, maybe mingle with some of the other participants and subtly ask a few of the right questions. The fact that the word "anonymous" was part of the name didn't faze me one bit.

Kiki brought me back to the present. "Yeah. I recognized her from some photos I saw in the papers a few years ago. She looked different, but I would never forget that name." Kiki ran her hands through her short hair. "I even talked to Jimmy's sponsor and he agreed with me that it was odd. I think maybe Jimmy was murdered."

"Do you think the mayor killed him? Or was it your boss? " I was starting to hyperventilate. This was more than I could handle.

"Not the mayor—he had no reason to knock off Jimmy. Jimmy and I didn't work for the same boss, but I think it's a good chance the competitor figured he stole the money."

"You have to tell the police."

"I can't go to the cops. No one will listen to me, and I've got a kid to take care of. I don't want to end up like Jimmy. You were nice to me in jail when you offered to check up on my daughter. I don't forget things like that. I'm here to tell you to watch your back." Kiki stood with her back to me now, gazing down at the people perusing the shops.

"I'll go to the police if I have to. Please tell me who he was working for," I begged.

Before Kiki could answer, the sound of a vehicle with wheels squealing reverberated off the garage wall. I gasped at the sight of the black Hummer, open full throttle and headed directly for us. Kiki turned at the sound and started running along the half wall toward her Navigator. My feet froze.

The Hummer peeled around a cement column and Kiki spun around on the wall, now screaming something at the top of her lungs. I couldn't make it out completely, but my brain seemed to register "Run, Jayne, Run," for that is what I did. I ran for all I was worth in the opposite direction of the Hummer corralling Kiki. As I ran, I heard screeching and a bloodcurdling scream from Kiki.

I hit the door leading to the stairwell at a full gallop and skimmed over at least a dozen steps on my way down. Around the third corner, I stumbled and fell, slamming against the cement wall. I scrambled back up with bloody knees and kept moving. When I hit the fifth set of stairs on my way down, my heel broke and, like the idiot I am, I stopped to pick it up. After all, those shoes cost me a night's wages and not even the threat of death would make me lose that heel. Blood dripping down my legs, I made it to the street level and ran right into Tami Lynn in front of the valet stand. The impact knocked us both to the ground.

"What are you doing?" she screeched at me.

"You have to help me. There's a crazy person on the top floor of the garage and he's going to kill my friend."

"Get off of me, you fool," Tami said, picking herself up and looking around to see if anyone was watching us.

I stood on shaking legs. Parking lot grit stuck to my bloody knees, and I had dropped my purse in the collision, spilling the contents on the pavement. "I need to find my cell phone and call the police."

"She grabbed my arm, digging her claw-like fingernails into the skin. "What have you done now?"

We were interrupted by a woman's screams on the next street over. Without another thought for Tami Lynn, I hobbled as fast as I could with one broken shoe towards the sound, certain in my gut it had something to do with Kiki.

A crowd gathered around something lying on the ground. I pushed my way through, and there lay Kiki. Half of her had landed on some bougainvillea bushes, their paper-thin petals ripped from the spiny branches. The bushes had partially broken her fall, but not enough to prevent her blood from staining the sidewalk. Kiki's other half had hit the sidewalk... hard.

I ran over to kneel by her side, "Kiki, talk to me. Hang in there, I'm sure an ambulance will be here soon."

"Kiki's eyes fluttered open for a second and, when she opened her mouth to speak, blood bubbled from her throat. "Jayne." She whispered grabbing my arm tightly.

"Yes, Kiki. Tell me who did this to you?" I begged.

"My kid. Take care of my kid."

"I will, Kiki. I'll find her. I promise."

"Jayne, watch your back. Beware the lady seller." Kiki's eyes rolled up and her head lolled to the side.

"Someone help her!" I screamed to the crowd gathered around.

Paramedics arrived in moments, and I was pushed out of the way while they desperately tried to revive Kiki. I stood in a daze, the sounds fading while onlookers bumped and pushed to get a better view of the maimed woman. The words she spoke as she stood looking at the people, trailed through my head. Empty people, all just trying to fill up the empty spaces with more things.

I heard snippets of conversation, theories about why she may have jumped off the top of the parking garage.

"No, she didn't jump. A car chased her over the edge," I mumbled to no one in particular.

"Hey, I saw you up there with her," said a woman pointing her diamond encrusted finger in my face.

Someone else yelled, "Did you push her?"

Someone tried to grab my arm from behind as another person shrieked, "Looks like you had a fight."

"No, she was my friend. I have a witness. Ask Tami Lynn, she knows I was trying to call the police after the Hummer chased us." I looked around for Tami Lynn, but she was nowhere in sight.

I didn't want to be accused of another murder, so I figured I better get out of there before the cops starting asking me questions. I had only one choice. I would have to retrieve my car from the garage.

I backed out of the crowd as they continued to shout

out theories, and walked as quickly as I could on wobbly legs. I didn't want to draw any more attention to myself. Stepping into the elevator, I received odd looks from several women in similar garb as myself, but without the broken shoe and bloody knees. They got off on the third level, leaving me to face the top level alone. I peered out cautiously, ready to push the close door button if necessary and take my chances on the street. There was no sign of the Hummer or any diabolical person slinking around the garage. I guessed that I only had a few minutes before the police cordoned off the scene below and sent someone up to this level. I forced my legs to move to the rental car and slid into the seat in my sweat-soaked clothes.

Without a backward glance, I threw the car in reverse and turned it toward the exit. As tempting as it was to floor it down the ramps, I had to proceed as if I didn't have a care in the world. I made it to level one before two police cars careened around the corner heading up. I barely paused to make sure I didn't plow down any pedestrians, and turned out of the garage onto the street. I don't remember the drive home except that Kiki's bloody face kept showing up in my mind, and my cheeks streamed with tears over the tragically horrible end to a rough life.

My apartment was dark and the absence of sound disheartening. I ran to the bathroom and retched until I couldn't breathe. I dropped my clothes on the floor and wrapped my robe around me. I needed a chocolate fix badly if I was going to deal with what had just happened. If I had a bottle of tequila I would have poured a shot... or two.

A woman who tried to help me wound up dead for her effort. There was no doubt in my mind that whoever ran me off the road was the same person who killed the mayor, and now Kiki. If I could find out who drove that car, I would be one step closer to solving this mystery.

CHAPTER FOURTEEN

Somehow I fell into a restless sleep on the sofa with the shopping channel on. When I awoke the next morning, I still had the remote clenched in my fist, but fortunately I didn't have a credit card in the other hand.

I was sore from head to toe. Still recovering from the car crash, my bruises had only started to fade. Both knees now sported scabs from flinging myself down six flights of stairs, and my neck was stiff from sleeping in a half upright position. Worse than the physical ailments, I was heartsick over watching poor Kiki die in front of me. What would happen to her daughter? Her mom was dead because of me. I was as responsible for Kiki's death as the person driving the vehicle. I would add this guilt to the already heavy burden I carried from my father's death.

It was essential that I remember each thing Kiki said before she died, but my neurons would not fire properly. I needed to admit I couldn't do this on my own. I called Bailey and, without filling her in on the details over the phone, told her I was heading her way for a major brainstorming session. Most importantly, we had to find Kiki's daughter and make sure she was okay.

When I got to Bailey's house, armed with a six-pack of Diet Mountain Dew, I told her everything I knew. This time I included all of the pertinent details, even the part about the money and almost being run over by a private jet.

"I'm so tired of trying to do this all by myself," I admitted.

"I should be really pissed off at you for leaving me out of the loop, but I can't stay mad at you for more than a few minutes." Bailey hugged me, "I'm so glad you're okay."

"I don't know how to find Kiki's daughter, or what I can possibly to say to her," I moaned.

"Do you think the police will want to question you for information about her death?"

"The only person at the scene who knew me was Tami Lynn, and she disappeared when the body was discovered. I have no reason to think they would make the connection, but I'm not going to give them one." I shuddered at the thought of more hours of interrogation by the abrasive

Detective Stewart.

"If you won't go to the police, then maybe we can have your attorney call the county morgue to see if they contacted someone to identify Kiki's body. From there we can hopefully trace her daughter and make sure she's okay," Bailey suggested.

I dug my attorney's business card out of my purse and left him a voice mail briefly describing what information I needed, without giving a reason.

"Let's go over what we know, and I'll take some notes."

We moved into her small office and, with two of her rescue dogs sleeping contentedly at our feet, got down to the business of putting the pieces of my life together. We commenced with the few days leading up to the last time I saw Franklin McArthur alive and finished with the events of last night. Bailey typed pages of notes, laid everything out before us and drew lines to connect events.

"Kiki told me she had seen Evangeline at NA meetings. She may have been there the night her ex-husband was killed. So, would she have had a chance to go to a meeting and then sneak over to his house? If not, that would give her a good alibi," I said, drawing a circle around her name. "Trent Hayworth claimed to have gone directly home, and I didn't see anyone on the road while I was walking.

Early the next morning he says he coached his son's softball game. That should be easy enough to verify."

"We don't know anything about who Kiki's boss is but, based on what she told you, we know two people rule the escort business in this town. Somehow, at least one of them is probably involved," Bailey added.

"And we can be pretty sure the Hummer person has something to do with Kiki's boss. Maybe a henchman?" I twirled a strand of my hair since I had no nails left to chew.

"A henchman? You need to stop watching scary movies late at night." Bailey slapped my hand to make me stop tugging my hair.

A chill ran up my spine. "Okay, an extremely bad man who doesn't hesitate to kill people."

"I'm going to write a program to process this in case we missed anything." Bailey's fingers flew over her keyboard. "I'm really sorry about Bugsy, too. I'm sure he'll turn up."

"If I knew he was okay, I wouldn't even care if I went to jail. Okay, that's not exactly true. I definitely don't want to go back to jail. But, he's out there somewhere, maybe hurt or hungry, and I haven't been able to do anything to find him."

"We'll find him together. I think it's a safe bet to say that whoever broke into your apartment was looking for something specific. Could have been the flash drive, the key for the locker, or maybe—not knowing about the locker—he or she was trying to find the cash. Until we have some more answers, I think we should start with what we do know. Let's make a plan for the day."

"Wait, I just remembered something. The night I was run off the road I went to the Rodeo Grounds because someone had left a note for me at the hostess stand." I described the note and the message instructing me to leave the bag."

"The mysterious bag of money." Bailey clapped her hands excitedly.

"So much has happened in the last few days, I totally forgot about the reason I was even on Leaping Lizard that night."

Bailey, always the pragmatist, broke our day into segments and I noticed in each group either she or Jonas was always by my side. She included Emmett, but he was questionable since he was always working or enjoying his busy social life. I started to wonder if my friends thought I was a total screw-up who couldn't do even the most mundane tasks on my own.

I pointed to her chart, where she listed my time allotment with Jonas. "Don't you think I should check with him before you commit him to babysit me?"

"He won't even know it. See, I've put him on the evening schedule. I think he'll be happy with that plan." She smiled mischievously. "You and I will check out the Little League schedule and try to verify Trent's alibi."

"Bailey, I can't ask you to spend every minute of your day watching over me."

"You didn't ask. This is non-negotiable."

"Geez, how did I get into this predicament?" I slouched in my chair like a teenager whose parent took away the car keys.

"You didn't ask for this. Most importantly, you're not alone."

"It was my lucky day when I accidentally ran into you with my cart at the pet food store." Realizing I had been solely focused on my troubles, and not a good friend lately, I asked, "How's life around here? Should I go pick up some supplies?"

"The four-legged kids and I are all fine, and you don't need to worry about us. For a change, let me do something for you."

"You got me out of jail. I don't know what I would have done if I had to stay there one more night." I shuddered at the memory.

Bailey scrolled through her notes on the monitor. "What about that list of names you mentioned with the money? Did it make any sense to you?"

"I haven't had time to think about it much, but I

know who quite of few of the people are."

We decided to get busy with what we could do now,
and logged on to the Internet to search the Little League
schedule. The website didn't list coaches' names, but did
include the schedule and location of games. Finding several
games occurring later in the day, we decided to hit the trail
and see if we would find Trent coaching at any of them.

We mapped out our course, and for fun, put all of the
addresses in my rental car's GPS, letting it tell us which route
was the best. In between, I left three more messages with my
attorney hoping for information on Kiki's daughter, or maybe
an update on my case.

We made our first stop at the Black Mountain
Ballpark, moved on to the Sonoran Heights Elementary
School, and finished up at the Desert Arroyo Middle School...
with Bailey gripping the dashboard hard enough that I
expected to see dents.

When we arrived at the Ballpark, we found a game
already underway. Locating a parking spot was more difficult
than taking a dinner order from a table full of children. After
fifteen minutes of driving around, we nabbed a spot when a
harried parent pulled out with a carload of screaming kids.

"Let's walk around by the bleachers first to see if we
see him. If he's here, maybe we can ask a few questions of the
parents," I suggested.

We strolled over as if to watch the game, all the while trying to look inconspicuous. We peered at the adults in the stands and on the field to see if Trent Hayworth was around. After spending another forty-five minutes checking and double-checking we agreed he was not at this game.

We moved on to the next location and repeated the process—me driving, Bailey hanging on as if her life depended on it. I started to get frustrated and lose hope that we could either eliminate Trent Hayworth or confirm he didn't have an alibi.

"We're not getting anywhere, and this whole day has been a waste of time," I said forlornly.

"We're already out, we may as well hit the last stop," Bailey suggested.

I hid my surprise at her willingness to keep driving around town, but pointed the car in the direction of our last stop.

We drove to the Desert Arroyo School and, even with the little car, were forced to park three blocks away. Parents milled about and undisciplined kids ran wild, high on sugary drinks. We were in luck as a game was in progress on the field.

Spying Trent on the far side by the dugout, we moved in closer. His team was on the field and the parents were going crazy in the stands. I noticed one woman in particular seemed venomous in her criticism of the other team. I pretended to wave at someone and moved up a few bleachers so I could sit right behind her. The next time she yelled her opinion, I echoed her comments, only louder.

She turned to look at me and smiled co-conspiratorially.

"That should have been a strike," I said to her. "Which one is yours?"

"He's the third baseman."

"He's cute. Has he been playing long?"

"Ever since he could hold the mitt. My husband pushed him into it, but now he loves it, and I never miss a game."

A bell started ringing in my head. This was my chance, but I had to be careful not to alert her to my purpose.

"This is my first game."

"Which boy is yours? I thought I knew all of the parents."

"Ah, my son's not here. I wanted to check out the teams first. We're new to the Valley," I ad libbed.

"Your son will love it. The Cactus Foothills teams are the best. We haven't lost a game since Trent took over coaching."

"Which one is he?" I asked playing dumb.

"The tall handsome one," she said giving me a wink.

Trying to keep the discussion on target, I asked, "Has he been coaching long?"

"He took over last season when the previous coach had too many work commitments. The kids have practice three times a week and games on the weekends, so we're here more than we're at home."

"When do they practice?" I asked, noticing for the first time that Trent was looking in my direction. I had been discovered, and he didn't look happy.

"Usually Monday, Wednesday, and Friday after school."

This was almost too easy, so I continued probing, "And then they have games every weekend?"

"They have to start early on the weekends because it's already starting to get hot. Plus, some of the parents help organize the equipment and carpool all the kids. The week before last a sprinkler problem flooded the field, so we had to play extra games over the weekend. We don't usually start at six-thirty in the morning, but we had so many teams needing to play it was exhausting."

I was trying to do the calculations in my head. If they started the games at six-thirty he would have had to sneak out of his house early. Could he have slipped away without his wife noticing before getting ready for the game? Would he have had time to leave the practice without being noticed and sneak up to the mayor's? I calculated the miles from here to the scene of the murder. I didn't think I could eliminate him entirely, but he had a strong alibi.

While pondering the logistics of how the mayor was murdered, a cheer went up from the crowd. I looked up to see what all the excitement was about only to see a black Hummer parked across the field. In a panic, I jumped up in time to stop a foul ball with my head. If I didn't know better I would swear Trent had orchestrated it. Stars exploded in my eyes and I tried to take a few steps to get to Bailey but my legs wouldn't cooperate. I tumbled down the wooden bleachers, thumping my head on the hard wood with each somersault.

Gagging at a strong odor, I realized someone was waving smelling salts under my nose. I forced my eyes open only to see Trent's face inches from my own.

"Here drink this." He pushed a bottle of water at me and leaned down close to my ear. "Just what do you think you're doing talking to my wife?" he hissed.

"Nothing!" I tried to yell, but with so much noise in my head I couldn't tell if I imagined it or had spoken out loud. The face of a handsome paramedic loomed in my vision and I could see his full luscious lips moving. In my mind, I was reaching up to him. His face became Jonas's and he was leaning down to kiss me and lifting me up into his arms. I closed my eyes.

When I opened them I was in a hospital bed with Jonas by my side.

"Oh, my head hurts," I said. "What happened?"

Jonas stood and took my hand. "You caught a fly ball with your head," he said.

"It wasn't intentional." I felt the lump on my forehead.

"If I ever take you to a baseball game, I'll be sure to put a catcher's mask on your face before the game starts."

"I swear that kid aimed the ball at me."

"You're getting yourself paranoid now. That was just a Little League kid who hit the ball wrong and you ended up with a mild concussion. Maybe more from taking a tumble down the bleachers than anything else." He brushed my hair out of my face.

"Where's Bailey?"

"She had to get home to feed the zoo, so I'm on duty. She said you would know what that means."

"How did she reach you?"

"I called your cell to check on you and she answered."

"Shouldn't you be at work?"

"I'm done for the day. Don't you remember we had a date tonight?"

"Oh yeah, we had a date," I replied meekly.

"You sure go to a lot of trouble to stand a guy up," he joked.

"Some days I wonder why I get out of bed." I suddenly felt self-conscious in my dreary hospital gown and bruised face. "Are you sure you still want that date?"

"I told you last night I knew you'd be a handful when I met you. I think I can make it the eight seconds it takes to get to the bell in this rodeo."

"Bailey and I were at that game trying to find the mayor's real killer."

"And you think it was an eight year old?"

"Very funny. No, I have reason to believe that Trent Hayworth may be involved. He was there at the game, coaching. I spoke to his wife, and I think he has a pretty solid alibi. Unfortunately." I glanced up at him. "You should go home. Nothing is going to happen to me here in the hospital. Even I should be safe for a few hours."

At that moment, the nurse came by to announce visiting hours were over and ushered Jonas out the door. He left feeling confident since I was confined to bed and, even I was unlikely to get into more trouble today. Obviously, he didn't know me that well—yet.

CHAPTER FIFTEEN

Mornings in a hospital seem to be much the same as they are all night. People talking, machines beeping, and someone disturbing you constantly to check your vital signs. They tell you to get some rest, and put in their best effort to keep you awake.

I managed to stumble into the small bathroom adjoining my private room and look in the mirror. It was an alarming sight. The bruises from my joy ride through the desert had barely faded and now I sported a knot on my forehead the size of a grapefruit. My green eyes were bloodshot and my nose looked like it had swollen to the size of a Toucan beak. My hair hung ratty and tangled and I was pretty sure I smelled bad.

I spoke to my reflection in the mirror. "Here's a fine

mess you've gotten yourself into. How do you manage to screw up whatever comes into your orbit? You can't even go to a little kid's softball game without winding up in the hospital. And, just wait until you get this bill!"

Calculating what my latest misadventure would cost motivated me to get myself dressed. I didn't want to think about what the hospital was charging me for each aspirin, or whatever it was they fed me. My insurance from the restaurant was limited, and the deductible was three thousand dollars. Unless I borrowed more from the money bag, I would be paying for this for the next two years. I needed to get out of the hospital and home where I could rest and try to clear my foggy brain. Something clattered around in my head like a dinner order I forgot to place, and I needed to find a spoonful of peace and quiet to pull it to the forefront.

I rummaged around in the wall-mounted closet and found my clothes. My cell phone held enough charge to, maybe, make one phone call before it died. There I go again, with only one phone call or I'm stuck in this different kind of jail. I didn't look at the hospital as a place to get well, but more as a place to suck the last of my finances out like an IV drip directly into their bank account. Dressed and ready to go before anyone came in to check my blood pressure one last time, with my head throbbing with each uncertain step, I tottered out to the nurse's station.

Looking up from a stack of medical charts, a crisply dressed nurse asked, "May I help you?"

"Yes, I'm checking out," I said as if I were leaving a hotel rather than the hospital.

"I beg your pardon?"

"I need to leave. Is there anything you need me to sign?"

She looked at me quizzically again and, realizing I was a patient, said sternly, "You can't check yourself out, the doctor must release you first."

"I can't afford to stay here. My insurance won't cover most of this bill, and I really just need to go home. I'll be fine," I argued.

"I'm sorry, but I can't authorize it." She stood, came around the nurse's station and took my arm as if to drag me back to my room."

"I didn't ask you to authorize it. I'm telling you I'm leaving and that's that." I replied, yanking my arm from her grasp.

I stomped off down the hall while she frantically called for a doctor to come to her assistance. I knew there was no way they could force me to stay and rack up expenses, so I figured I better keep moving while I still had the nerve. Normally, it wouldn't take much for me to back down in the face of someone else's authority, but it was time to cowgirl up. Time was running out and, if I didn't uncover the true killer's identity soon, another person could end up dead. So far, three people may have been murdered, a teenager was left without her mother, my cat was missing, and all I had done was confirm the alibis of others, leaving me still as the prime suspect. I was missing something, and I had a promise to keep to Kiki. I needed to find her daughter and make sure she was okay.

I found my way out of the maze of hospital corridors to the front entrance only to discover a sky black as night with ominous rain clouds. I jumped as a loud clap of thunder announced the arrival of an off-season storm. In the distance, the makings of a wall of dust formed. Fortunately, I carried cash in my wallet from my money-bag loan. It allowed me to call a cab to take me back to the school where my car remained, without alerting Jonas or Bailey.

When I got home, I saw a small pair of golden eyes peering out of my elderly neighbor's drapes. For just a second, I swore it was Bugsy, but I blinked and the eyes were gone. More than likely... just my imagination running wild. I wondered if she had come across any clues as to Bugsy's whereabouts in her daily walks, but I would have to wait to talk to her later, after I showered and organized my plans for the day.

I couldn't remember who was supposed to babysit me

this morning, so I called Bailey and Jonas. Thankful to get voicemail for them both, I left messages that I had been released and was home resting.

I turned on my old desktop computer and, while it took its time warming up, I popped open my own version of an IV, a diet soda. I munched on a doughnut, which somehow managed to find its way into my shopping cart with the healthy food. I considered that maybe I should have asked Jonas to bring me home so he could have made me another lovely breakfast while I lounged on the sofa.

Stripping out of my day-old clothes, I took a quick shower, wrapped myself in my robe, and stepped into my soft fuzzy slippers. Sitting down at the computer, I made myself a To Do list. First, I needed to try to find Kiki's daughter. Second, I needed to review the names from the money bag to see if I could find any association between them. Third, I needed to figure out what Kiki meant by the "lady seller."

Obviously, she was talking about a madam who made a good living off of the escort services her employees provided. I figured if she had one-hundred-thousand dollars in a gym bag, she probably stashed more money someplace else. How had Franklin McArthur come to possess it? If I assumed the list of names was her client list, maybe she was willing to kill to get it back.

From what I knew of the mayor, it was entirely

possible he was blackmailing her. Maybe the money was actually a payoff to get him to keep his silence. Remembering how he had blackmailed Trent Hayworth, he was certainly capable of it. Or, was he actually blackmailing someone on the list, and that person was the killer? Why then kill Kiki and the young man in the photos with Trent? I was pretty sure whoever the killer was, he or she was affiliated in some way with the prostitution ring.

The ear-splitting barking of my cell phone startled me out of my reverie. I hesitated a moment, knowing it was Bailey, probably calling to check up on me.

"Hey, sorry about the softball game. Who won?" I said trying to divert her from asking why I left the hospital so early, but knowing it was probably futile.

"Very funny. I'm surprised you are home from the hospital already." She was not to be deterred on her mission.

"I had to get out of there. Do you know what they charge just to take your temperature?" I asked.

"I know it's outrageous but, despite that, you're not supposed to be alone. I'll be right over."

"I'm perfectly safe here and there's something you can do for me from home with all your super computers. Do you think you could find out Kiki's last name, and maybe where she lived? I need to make sure her daughter is okay. Kiki said she was a teenager and she shouldn't be alone at a time like this. My useless attorney hasn't even called me back yet."

"Hmmm. I'll see what I can do. Did Jonas stay at the hospital with you last night?"

"They threw him out once visiting hours were over."

"So, do you remember the paramedic who treated you at the game? He asked me out. My friend is lying there unconscious, and the guy hits on me," she said with surprise and a touch of delight.

"I thought I dreamed him. Is he really cute with brown eyes and nice lips?"

"Yep, that's Ben."

"So, did you say yes?"

"I said maybe. I haven't been out on a date in one hundred years. I'm not sure I remember what to do."

"You do what Emmett always tells me to do. You get your flirt on and have some fun."

"We'll see." I could hear the smile in her voice coming through the phone lines.

"I'm so happy for you."

"We'll see," she said again.

Getting back to the topic at hand, I said "I think we agree whoever killed Franklin McArthur also killed Kiki and her friend from the escort service. Now we just have to narrow it down from the list of names in the money bag, or figure out who the madam is. I started to look up all the escort services in the valley, but do you know there are over fifty of them?"

"I guess you could start calling and asking for Kiki, but whoever runs it probably already knows she's dead."

"I thought that, too, but what other choices do I have?"

We hung up with Bailey vowing to find Kiki's daughter and me with my long list of "gentleman-friendly" service providers to go through. If I could find out which one Kiki worked for, I could make an anonymous call to the police, ask them to look into Kiki's death, and hope they could tie it all in together. There was still a chance they wouldn't believe me, but it was all I had. I wondered if her death had been classified as a suicide or as what it was—murder.

After an hour of methodically running through the phone book of Maricopa County-area escort services—listings with names from A Date with a Model to Tender Loving Care—I decided to look at the photos again. Even though the sight of Trent's naked hairy body repulsed me, I felt I had missed something.

I clicked through the images one by one trying to focus on the less obvious parts of the photos. When I looked at the one photo with the reflected image of the photographer's hand, something fell into place in my brain. I knew where I had seen that hand or, more specifically, the large diamond ring on the hand. I saw the same ring the night the mayor died, only then I had been too preoccupied dealing with its wearer to think about the symbolism of it.

When I first saw the somewhat blurry image on my monitor, I thought it was the letter "S." Now that I remembered it more clearly, I knew it wasn't a letter but the shape of a snake—a rattlesnake. Two blood-red rubies marked the eyes, a body of diamonds coiled around the finger and finished in the slightly raised tail rattle. I remembered seeing the ring on Tami Lynn's hand when she gave me my pay the night of the mayor's cocktail party.

I started to connect the pieces. Someone in the restaurant had mentioned she ran a real estate firm. Was Tami Lynn an escort posing as an agent? Is that how she was able to afford her regular BOTOX injections and designer clothes? She could be the link between the mayor and the madam. I shook my head in amazement and chewed on my lower lip.

Mentally and physically exhausted despite numerous Dews, I settled on the sofa for a short break with the shopping channel on and fell into a sleep disturbed by dreams of lost kitties, people falling off buildings, and for sale signs.

Hours later, I woke to the sound of my cell phone

ringing. Since it wasn't barking at me, I knew it wasn't Bailey with an update. Still groggy, I answered on the fifth ring.

"Hi darlin', how are you feeling?" A deep sexy voice inquired.

Jonas. I stretched slowly, trying to get the kinks out, and tentatively put a hand to my forehead. "I'm still alive, so maybe that in itself is a good thing," I responded.

"I'm wrapping up work for the day, so I thought maybe you would like something to eat."

At the mention of food my stomach growled. "I can't remember when I last ate anything."

"We still have a date to go on."

I wasn't sure I was up to going out in public in my current state, but I really didn't want to be alone for another night.

Jonas must have sensed my hesitation. "How about if I pick you up and bring you over here. I can throw some steaks on the grill and we can watch a movie."

"Sounds like heaven."

"Great. I'll be over in an hour. Can you wait that long?"

"It won't be easy, but I'll manage."

"Have a piece of the fruit you bought to hold you over, but don't spoil your dinner with chocolate," he warned.

How did that guy know me so well already? Despite

his food warnings, I was thinking it would be hard to wait long enough to see him again. I desperately needed the diversion, and couldn't resist clapping my hands in excitement about something good happening in my life for a change.

Moving slowly and stiffly I gently applied enough make-up to cover some of the bruises. What to wear was more of a quandary. After digging through my closet and trying on five different outfits, I settled for jeans and bedazzled t-shirt. So, perhaps the top was a little low cut in the front, and maybe a bit snug, but I hoped it would divert his gaze from the condition of my face. I put the finishing touches on just as Jonas knocked on the door.

He gave a long whistle as I opened the door. "You do clean up nice."

I laughed despite my sore face, "I'm glad you approve."

"Ready to go?"

"More than ready, I'm starving."

I grabbed my purse and locked the bleak, empty apartment behind me. Habit made me turn to look back as we walked to his truck. No eyes peered at me from my window. Tomorrow, I needed to check the animal shelters again to see if anyone had found Bugsy. As smart as he was, I didn't think he could make it long as an outside cat.

Jonas opened my door, and I was slightly surprised not to see Molly already occupying the passenger seat. I looked questioningly at him.

"Molly stayed home and she wasn't happy about it at all," he said laughing.

"I'll save some scraps and make it up to her," I promised.

Jonas lived a few miles outside of the town limits on a modest plot of land. He owned a one-story house he built with his own hands, which was approximately half the size of the open-sided pole barn he built for his horses. Each time I turned the page of who he was, I liked him even more.

"Be it ever so humble," he said modestly opening the knotty alder front door. "Welcome to my small slice of heaven."

In a glance, I observed the western theme running throughout: the worn leather sofa, the hammered copper and pine console cabinet containing a large flat-screen television, the Native American patterned rugs scattered over the Mexican tile floors. The decor was masculine, but still managed to feel homey and comfortable. Not one handmade leather pillow looked out of place, no dirty dishes littered the kitchen sink and, as he gave me a brief tour, I could see his bed, made perfectly.

I pictured my apartment filled with thrift store, hand-me-down furniture where no two pieces made a set, and the constant state of disarray. I could appreciate someone else's sense of style, but most days wondered if my outfits matched, let alone coordinated my surroundings.

"It's not what I expected," I said honestly.

"What did you expect?"

"I'm not sure, maybe something not so perfect."

Jonas laughed, "I don't take credit for the decorating. I have a client who volunteered her expertise. Would you feel better if I messed it up a little?"

"Yes, definitely!"

"Don't put any ideas in my head. I'm trying to be a gentleman."

"Maybe we should focus on dinner. As you requested, I was good and didn't eat any chocolate."

"That means I should get busy in the kitchen. Make yourself comfortable and I'll get you a glass of wine."

"Is there anything I can do to help?"

"Nope, I'm all set. Are you taking any pain killers for the lump on your head?"

"No, I didn't get any prescriptions from the doctor." I didn't want to admit to Jonas I had left the hospital before the doctor had a chance to prescribe anything.

"Great, I have a nice bottle of Cabernet I've been saving for a special occasion, and this seems like a good night to sample it."

A little fluttery feeling danced around in my stomach. I wasn't sure if it was merely hunger, or whether Jonas gave me butterflies. I couldn't remember the last time a man had opened a special bottle of wine, let alone cooked dinner for me.

I wandered around the living room with Molly following at my heels as if she wanted to make sure I didn't feel lonely, or maybe to ensure I didn't make a mess. It was odd having someone wait on me for a change.

Jonas handed me a glass of wine and I gave my customary cowboy toast before we clinked glasses and each took a sip.

One benefit of working in an upscale restaurant was the required wine tastings. We offered a hundred wines by the glass. My memory skills came in handy when recognizing the unique flavors of each, and knowing what wine to pair with what entrée. This wine was full bodied and tasted of dark cherry and black currant with hints of oak and cinnamon.

"This will be delicious with beef. You made a great choice." I took another sip, allowing the wine to roll around in my mouth, savoring the flavors dancing on my tongue.

"Just relax and we'll eat in a few minutes."

"I'm not sure I remember how to relax with all that's been going on," I admitted.

"I think you've earned a night off." Jonas pointed a remote from the open kitchen towards the living room and his stereo came on, playing my favorite George Strait song.

I took a deep drink of my wine and focused on George singing about making it to Amarillo by morning with only what he had on his back and the one goal to make it in time for the next rodeo. My body relaxed in small increments and I allowed myself to sink deeper into the buttery-soft leather. I could get used to this.

A few songs later, Jonas announced, "Dinner's ready. I hope you like your steak medium, because I only know how to cook it one way."

"Sounds perfect." My mouth watered at the delicious smells wafting through the house.

Jonas led the way to the small dining room adjacent to the kitchen. A single candle flickered in the center of a rustic pine table. Jonas pulled out a leather-backed chair for me and I was struck by the mural of running horses painted on the wall opposite me.

"The painting is beautiful. Did your decorator do that, too?" A tiny part of me was starting to get jealous of this decorator friend of his.

"My mother painted it. She painted the design on the table, too, after I made it."

"You made this table? You really are a man of many

talents." I couldn't help running my hands over the smooth wood in appreciation. "Is there anything you can't do?"

"Quite a few things actually. If you must know, this is the only thing I know how to cook well enough to serve to a guest."

I breathed a sigh of relief. "Thank goodness, because you were starting to seem too perfect, and I was feeling a little intimidated."

Jonas laughed, and we dug into New York bone-in strip steaks, baked potatoes with crispy skins from the grill, a Caesar salad and, horror of horrors, peas. I hated peas with an intensity that would boil water. This would necessitate creativity on my part, but I had years of practice at my mother's table in moving food around without eating it.

"This is the best meal I've had in ages," I said between mouthfuls, scattering the peas around to look as if there were fewer on my plate

"It's nice to see a woman who has an appetite and isn't afraid to eat." Jonas pushed the salad bowl in my direction encouraging me to help myself to more. "You don't like peas?"

"Ah, sure I do," I forked a mouthful in and swallowed them whole. "If I don't stop now, I'll have to unzip my jeans." I slapped my hand over my mouth, realizing too late I probably shouldn't have said exactly what was on my mind.

Jonas smiled with a glint in his eyes, "That's always an option."

I smiled, deciding to keep my mouth shut rather than give voice to what bad Jayne was whispering in my ear about messing up his perfectly made bed. I helped clean up the kitchen and we moved, with the remainder of the wine, to the back patio.

Without any streetlights to interfere, the stars glittered in the sky above me, flawlessly bestowing a soft light over the desert. The air was cooler and a slight breeze carried the perfume of jasmine and desert lavender. A short distance away, the horses snorted occasionally and shifted positions in their pens, as they settled down for the night. Not wanting to spoil the natural beauty of the moment, instinctively Jonas and I sat side by side on the log porch swing, quietly hypnotized.

I shuddered as a chill passed over me when thoughts of my predicament crept back into my head. Jonas moved a little closer wrapping his arm around my shoulders. If only I could stay in this place forever and forget all the stuff jumbled in my head, except for the way I felt at this moment—safe in the arms of a cowboy.

CHAPTER SIXTEEN

I must have allowed myself to relax enough to doze off, or perhaps it was the second bottle of wine we polished off while watching the old John Wayne western, because the next thing I knew someone was snoring, loudly. Waking with a start, to my embarrassment, I realized it was me.

Jonas had dozed off beside me with his other arm around Molly, who was nestled on the edge of the sofa, claiming her spot as his best girl. I gently slid out from under his arm so as not to wake him. I sat upright and watched him sleeping beside me. I gently trailed my finger over his soft lips. What turn of fate had brought him into my life?

I liked the way the smile danced across his face, and the way the creases in the corners of his eyes showed he had weathered a few storms before hurricane Jayne swept into his life. I liked the solidness of his chest when he put his arms around me, and the way his face was a little scruffy from needing a shave. My body was giving me signals and, despite the fact that I knew my sensibilities had been dulled by the wine, all I could think about was how nice it would be to see Jonas with nothing on but a towel wrapped loosely around his hips after a steamy shower. Or maybe just lazing across his bed with only a sheet draped over him, or maybe with only his cowboy hat on, or maybe...

Jonas awoke, startling me out of my fantasy. "Sorry, I must have fallen asleep. Some date I am."

I stretched my aching limbs, "I'm surprised you could sleep with me snoring away."

He laughed, and there were those creases again making my pulse quicken. "If I didn't know what your last few days had been like, I would think it was my company."

"This has been the perfect evening and I don't really want to go home, but I think we better start moving in that direction." Good Jayne was back, darn her.

"Don't take this the wrong way, but after a second bottle of wine I'm not sure driving is a good idea."

My eyes wandered to his bedroom and those dangerous thoughts tiptoed back to the forefront. Involuntarily, I licked my lips, my throat suddenly dry. I stood intent on taking this evening in the direction of romance, but my legs felt wobbly and the room started to spin.

"I don't feel good."

"You're looking a little green. Maybe you should sit back down."

I slapped my hand over my mouth and ran to the bathroom, making it just in time to lose my dinner in the toilet, whole peas and all. I retched until there was nothing left in my stomach. Jonas stood behind me holding my hair out of the way, and then wiped my face with a cool cloth. What is worse, having the man you thought about dancing between the sheets with see you throw up, or having him see you throw up the peas you didn't chew?

"Come on let me put you to bed, darlin'." He half led, half carried me into his pristine bedroom. I didn't have the strength to argue when he pulled my shirt over my head, tugged off my jeans and tucked me gently in his comfy bed, laying the cloth over my forehead. He turned off the lights and quietly closed the door.

I awoke to the sun warming my face and wet kisses on my cheek. I opened one eye to stare into Molly's shaggy face just as she was getting ready to plant a big one on my mouth.

"Ugh, Molly stop. It's too early and my head hurts way too much to fight you off." I tried to crawl out from under her weight without moving more than necessary.

My head throbbed and my throat was sore. I could hear Jonas moving around in the living room and wondered where he slept last night. I didn't remember much after he put me to bed, but did have enough sense this morning to be embarrassed that he had seen me partially undressed. Oh no, even worse he had seen me throwing up.

On the bedside table, Jonas had placed a bottle of aspirin and a glass of water. I sat up and gingerly swung my legs over the side of the bed. Just being vertical eased the hammering in my head. I popped three aspirin and washed them down with all of the water. My top and jeans lay neatly folded at the foot of the bed. Moving in super slow motion so as not to aggravate the cattle drive stampeding through my brain, I dressed. Mentally I berated myself for having the third, or was it the fourth, glass of wine. It might not have been the best decision after taking a softball to the head.

I shuffled out of the bedroom preparing to face Jonas, only to find he had stepped outside to tend to his horses. I stood in his kitchen looking out the window to see him carrying on a conversation as he curried one of his horses in the pen. Despite my hangover, I couldn't stop grinning like an idiot. Molly whined at the door, eager to be part of whatever Jonas was up to.

I slipped into my sandals and followed her out.

"Good morning," I said standing back a ways from Jonas and the horse.

"Morning sleepy head. You don't have to stand back there. Tulsa is the gentlest horse you'll ever find."

"It's not Tulsa I'm worried about," I said holding my hand over my mouth and trying to check how disgusting my breath was. "You wouldn't happen to have an extra toothbrush lying around I could borrow?"

Jonas chuckled. "How do you feel?"

I looked down at the ground and felt the heat rising to my cheeks, "Like I chewed dirt and got kicked in the head." After a pause, I added, "Mortified."

"I take full blame for opening the second bottle of wine."

"I'm a big girl, I didn't have to drink it." I desperately wanted to broach the subject of the undressing part of the evening, but thought maybe I should pretend that part didn't happen.

"Do you feel up to taking a ride?"

"I would love to, but I'm not really dressed for it."

Jonas looked at me, his eyes slowly moving from my sandaled feet to my snug top.

"What?" I asked looking down at myself to see if I had my top on inside out or backwards.

"I was just thinking of how you were dressed when I

put you to bed last night."

Rarely was I rendered completely speechless, but this was a blue ribbon moment.

He laughed, gave Tulsa a pat on the rump, and walked over to me to put his arm around my shoulders and lead me toward the house. "Come on, silly girl, let's try to rustle up a toothbrush for you, and I'll make some breakfast if you feel up to eating."

Finding my voice, I answered though still covering my mouth with my hand, "I always feel up to eating when someone else is cooking."

Jonas dug in his bathroom cabinet and came up with a toothbrush, courtesy of his last visit to the dentist, and left me to freshen up while he made breakfast.

I swear there is nothing in the world better than someone fixing you a big breakfast after too much alcohol. Truth be told, someone taking care of me in any situation was quite nice. I could definitely get used to this. After breakfast, Jonas took me home so I could call the animal shelters to see if there was any information on Bugsy.

I didn't tell him the more important mission was to try to talk to Tami Lynn to see what information she might give me. If she was willing to tell me who the madam was, I could certainly use the information to go to the police. Maybe then they would consider someone besides me as the likely murderer. Of course, if she was deeply involved in some sort of blackmail ring, she may not want to talk to me at all. I looked again at the list of names which had been tucked in the gym bag. If the police wouldn't listen to me, perhaps I could go to the media with this list.

As I sat deep in thought about this latest direction, my cell phone rang. The caller ID was blocked, so I hoped it was someone calling about my cat.

"Hello."

"Is this Jayne Stanford?" said a slightly familiar woman's voice.

"Yes," I said, trying to recall where I had heard the voice.

"I realized who you were after you left the mayor's office the other day."

That's where I recognized the timid tones from... the mayor's assistant. "Hi, Sheila." I couldn't imagine why she would call me, but prayed it wasn't to tell me she was reporting the incident to the police after all.

"I don't think you killed him, and I may have an idea of who did. Can you meet me at the Cave Creek Coffee Company in a half hour?"

"I'll be there."

"Come alone."

I hung up the phone, feeling more confused than

ever, and with a strong feeling of déjà vu. After what happened the last time someone demanded I come alone, I thought I should at least let someone know where I was headed, but then chuckled at my paranoia. After all, what could possibly happen at a coffee shop?

I grabbed my purse and rushed out the door. This time, I vowed to be the first one to arrive. Besides, they had amazing baked goods, so I may as well get some extra caffeine and enjoy a cheese Danish while I waited.

Getting there in record time, I checked out the parking lot for a Hummer hovering nearby. With an all-clear, I went in and grabbed a table by the window, figuring I could keep an eye out for Sheila, as well as watch out for any potential trouble on the outside.

She arrived only a few minutes after me, her soft-soled shoes barely making a sound on the tile floor, and slid quietly into the seat opposite. Anyone seeing the two of us could have done a study in the contrast. Me—all wild, curly locks of hair spiraling in all directions, still wearing last night's clothes and, I'm embarrassed to admit, last night's underwear, too, with no time for a shower before she called. Sheila—in her somber knee-length gray skirt and white oxford shirt buttoned all the way up, she would have fit perfectly in a library. . Her large glasses gave her the appearance of being either an intellectual or partially blind. I reminded myself that sometimes you had to be more vigilant with the ones who appeared reserved.

"Hi, Sheila." I took a small sip of the green tea I purchased to offset the unhealthy calories in my cinnamon streusel muffin.

She sat for a moment taking deep breaths and studying her hands, folded in her lap. Finally, she looked up at me, "I loved him, you know."

My instinct was to ask who, but thankfully I chewed my muffin for a minute and realized she meant the mayor. "I'm sorry for your loss, but I promise I didn't kill him. Did you know he wasn't one of the good guys?"

"He wasn't all bad. It was that other woman who made him do those things."

"What other woman?"

"The whore," she spat out the word as if it burned her tongue. "She turned him against me."

"Maybe you could start from the beginning and tell me what happened between you and the mayor." The only words I wanted to hear from her was who she thought killed him, but my instinct told me to let her go at her own speed.

Sheila described how she had been working for the incumbent mayor of the town for years when she first met Franklin McArthur. For her, it was love at first sight. He was still married to Evangeline at the time, but when their affair started Franklin assured her his marriage was over. He told her of his wife's addiction to painkillers and how difficult it was to leave her.

She was so in love that she helped him get elected by passing along the incumbent's strategy and a few choice tidbits of scandal. Once elected, she remained as the mayor's assistant, and they continued to carry on the affair in secret. When Evangeline's family money ran out and they were divorced, Sheila was sure he would marry her. But the wedding never came to fruition and, before long, he started avoiding her outside of the office.

I leaned closer to Sheila as her voice dropped to a whisper.

"I started following him to see what he was doing when he told me he was working late on town business."

"And you found he was cheating on you," I guessed.

"He was with that whore. I begged him to come to my church, but she pulled him away from me." Her hands fluttered around her throat and I suspected she wore a religious symbol under the buttoned up neckline. I hoped her faith would help her recover from the damage the mayor had done to her.

"Were you angry with him?"

"I told you I loved him. I would have done anything for him if only..."

"If only he would have married you?"

"If only he had lived. I know he did bad things, but she made him do it."

"If he was cheating on me, I would have been mad enough to do something about it," I volunteered, hoping it would prompt her to confess, if she was the killer.

"I didn't kill Franklin."

"So who do you think did?" I started to wonder where this discussion was going.

"When you came into his office that day, I didn't recognize you. Later on, I saw your picture and it didn't make sense to me."

"The police seem to think I had enough reason, but I swear to you, it wasn't me." I didn't know why I felt compelled to defend myself to Sheila, but she might be my only chance to clear my name. Besides I wasn't totally sure she didn't have the best motive of all—jealousy.

"It could have been that whore. He told me he had one more big deal to wrap up and then we could leave town and he would marry me."

The words to ask her if she believed him balanced on the tip of my tongue, but instead I asked, "Do you know what the deal was?"

"No, he never shared any of his business dealings with me which weren't directly related to the work in the mayor's office."

"What was his relationship to Tami Lynn Carroll?"

"Is she the blonde with the big, you know, um, chest?"

"Yes, I think she might have been involved with the mayor."

I'm not sure how she fit in, but she wasn't the woman I saw him with."

"You mean the woman he was having an affair with? Do you know her name?"

A scornful laugh escaped her, "Her real name is Christine, but she goes by the name of Poppy."

"How would I find her?"

"Just ask her mother."

I knitted my brow, trying to make sense of what she was saying, "Who is her mother?"

"Why Franklin's housekeeper of course."

I flashed back to the night when Franklin had tried to molest me. What had the housekeeper said to me? A warning of some sort, which really didn't register until right now.

"Thanks, you've been a big help." I needed to make one last trip to the mayor's house, and this time I would not leave without some answers.

CHAPTER SEVENTEEN

Before I went to the mayor's house, I decided a quick shower and change of clothes would be a good idea. As I was getting out of the shower, my phone buzzed with a text from Bailey saying she had information on Kiki.

I quickly dialed her number. "Did you track down Kiki's daughter?" I asked before she had a chance to say hello.

"Not exactly, but I did read today's paper, and there is an article about the accident on page six."

I rarely watched the news on television, let alone actually stop moving long enough to read a paper.

Bailey continued, "The paper says the police consider it an accidental death at this point, but are still looking for a woman of interest. I think that may be you."

"Oh no, could this situation get any worse?" I cried.

"It also says there is a funeral service this afternoon at Brightview cemetery. I think we should go and see if we can talk to her daughter."

I had only been to one funeral in my life, and still experienced the nightmares it caused. I shuddered at the thought, but knew I had no choice. I had to keep my promise to Kiki, and if it meant going to her funeral to find her daughter, that is what I would do.

Bailey and I hung up after deciding what time I should pick her up. I sat down on the sofa, wishing my kitty was there for me to cuddle and to listen to my woes. I had no motivation to talk to the mayor's housekeeper, even though I knew it needed to be done. Instead, I turned on the shopping channel, my diversion of choice, and watched as hands with perfectly manicured nails enticed me to purchase all manner of rings with sparkling gemstones.

Eventually, I dragged myself off the sofa and started the process of digging through my closet to find suitable funeral attire. By the time my bed possessed all of the clothing I owned, I had narrowed the selection down to a slightly-too-short black cocktail dress or my black work pants with a pale lilac blouse. I felt Kiki would have appreciated the cocktail dress, but I wasn't so sure it was appropriate for the first time I met her daughter.

I checked my phone to see if there were any messages from Jonas, but remembered he was going to take his horse out for a ride. Disappointed, and wishing for another distraction, I decided to knock on my neighbor's door to see if she had seen any sign of my kitty on her daily walks.

I knocked and waited for a response. I was sure I heard someone moving around inside, but there was no answer. I tried the doorbell, and worried that perhaps something had happened to her. Moments later, she cracked the door, leaving the security chain in place.

"Hi, I'm your neighbor Jayne. Do you remember we talked the other day when I was looking for my cat?"

She stared at me as if I were a serial killer. I wondered if she was the type to watch the local news, or had seen something about her crazy neighbor and the mayor in the paper.

"Can I help you?" she asked suspiciously.

"I wondered if you might have seen my cat while doing your daily walk. You said you would keep an eye out for him."

"No, I haven't. Please leave me alone." She slammed the door in my face.

Stunned, I stood on her doorstep, wondering if all of my neighbors felt the same way, and if I would soon be getting a notice to vacate the premises. I wondered again why

I had taken that side job at the cocktail party. Then I remembered I hadn't been given much of a choice in the matter.

With my head hanging and my shoulders hunched, I walked slowly back to my apartment, barely registering the storm clouds lining up on the horizon. No sign of Bugsy meant he might have already become a coyote's late night snack. I couldn't endure the thought of him being gone—yet another death on my hands.

Back in my apartment I dressed, tugged, pinned, and stuffed my hair into a respectable updo, and applied make-up. I wanted to make the best first impression on Kiki's daughter I could.

On the way to pick up Bailey, I stopped at a grocery store and purchased a small bouquet of flowers. I didn't know how many mourners would be at Kiki's funeral, but I couldn't stomach the thought of her not having any flowers for her casket. No matter what her life may have been like, for a brief time she was a friend to me.

Bailey and I drove around the cemetery expecting a small gathering of mourners, standing solemnly by a gravesite. Instead, what we found was a Mardi Gras celebration complete with a brass band.

Eyes wide, we merged into the rear of the party hoping to blend in but standing out like two mules in a herd of zebras. Brightly colored costumes were the most prominent, and I counted at least three versions of Madonna, a Barbra Streisand, someone who looked like Barbara Bush, and four versions of Elvis at different times of his life. The band played a rousing rendition of "Amazing Grace" and a few mourners sang along at the top of their voices. On the opposite side of the group, the dress code focused more on the cleavage and less on the fabric.

I blinked at the glare of the polished gold hardware on the glimmering white casket. The small bouquet of carnations in my hand wilted in comparison to the array of flowers of every size, shape and color surrounding Kiki's remains like ladies in waiting. The scent of freshly mown grass tickled my nose.

Bailey nudged me and pointed to where a beautiful young woman stood in her modest black dress which was one size too large. Her head bowed, she mouthed words only Kiki would hear. Her hands shredded the tissue she held, allowing the pieces to flutter to the ground like snowflakes.

No words could ease her heartbreak. Nothing I could do could erase the events which brought about her mother's untimely death. Across the casket from me, she slowly raised her eyes and they seared my soul. I owed this girl my life and her future.

With a slight tilt of her head she beckoned me and I

approached in a trance. I weaved through the celebrity impersonators to stand before her my heart heavy.

"You must be Jayne," she said softly. "I'm Jenny. My mom told me she met someone in jail who fits your description and, since I know everyone else here, that leaves you."

"I'm so sorry about your mom. I know what it's like to lose a parent."

"Mom said you were nice to her and she wanted to help you out. She told me she was going to meet you the night she died."

"She did help me and it's my fault she died." I started to cry.

"Mom lived a dangerous life. It's the only thing we ever argued about."

The singing ended and Jenny took my hand as one of the Elvis impersonators stepped forward to speak. His melodious voice painted a picture of the bond between Kiki and Jenny as she squeezed my fingers tightly. A vision of the life they had shared flashed through my mind. I owed a debt to this girl that I could never repay.

After the service ended, we marched slowly behind the band as they played a rendition of The Beatles, All You Need is Love. Bailey and I were invited to join everyone for a reception at the apartment Jenny had lived with her mother.

"That was an interesting service," Bailey remarked as we followed the line of cars leaving the cemetery.

"I don't have much to compare it to. The only other funeral I've ever been to was for my father and it was a blur."

"What do you think will happen to Jenny now that she's on her own?"

"It's my fault her mother is dead. If Kiki hadn't tried to help me she would be alive right now and that might be me in the casket."

"You can't blame yourself. Kiki asked you to meet her there. Obviously either you or Kiki were followed by the murderer."

"I need to go talk to the Mayor's housekeeper. I think she may have some information about what happened that night that she isn't telling the police."

"Just be careful. I really don't want to attend another funeral anytime soon," Bailey warned.

"I am worried about Jenny being alone after everything that has happened. Maybe we should go to the police after all?"

"Let's find out if she has anyone to stay with her. If we go to the police she might be put in foster care. Didn't you say she is only a teenager?"

"Yes. Kiki told me her daughter was seventeen and hasn't graduated high school yet."

"Hmmm."

We were quiet as I negotiated the traffic and tried to keep the procession in my sight. My heart heavy about the circumstances surrounding Kiki's untimely death. Bailey looked out the window lost in her own thoughts.

I followed the cars as they turned into a two story apartment complex situated adjacent to a boarded up strip of retail shops. Each building in the complex was anchored by a lonely palm tree which dangled dried fronds as if too weary to make the effort to disengage them. I squeezed my clown rental next to a sun bleached two door sedan with a flat tire and dents in the hood. My car, Betsy would fit perfectly in this neighborhood.

Bailey and I brought up the rear of the crowd and wedged into the modest first floor apartment Jenny had shared with her mother. Sounds of smooth jazz were swirling around the room and my restaurant-tuned sense of smell detected roast chicken with rosemary. Despite the stressful situation, my mouth watered at the prospect.

Jenny sat on the paisley sofa surrounded by well-wishers, so we wandered into the kitchen. Snippets of conversation swirled around me. Stories of Kiki's generosity to everyone she met made it clearer why she tried to help me. I gazed into the crowded living room wondering what would happen to Jenny now that she was alone. Bailey's question rang in my ears. Where would she stay now if she couldn't be here? Was Jenny safe from whoever had killed her mother? I needed to keep my word to Kiki and make sure that her daughter would be okay.

At seventeen, she was too young to be on her own. Bailey's eyes caught mine and I was sure the same thoughts were running through her mind. She raised her eyebrows and tilted her head toward Jenny. I nodded my understanding.

As soon as an opportunity presented, we took position on either side of Jenny.

"Jenny, I know this is all very sudden but do you have somewhere to go? Some family nearby?" Bailey asked.

Jenny shrugged her shoulders. "No, there was no one but Mom and me. I haven't thought about what happens next. There was so much to do with planning the funeral and organizing everything."

"I promised your mom I would look out for you," I said.

"I'll be okay."

Jenny's words didn't match the confusion and loss reflected in her eyes. Before I could suggest that she come stay with me, Bailey offered her home.

"I have room at my place. That is, if you don't mind sharing the space with a few dogs, cats, a bird, a ferret and a few other four legged critters."

Jenny smiled, "I've always wanted a dog. Mom was allergic and the apartments we lived in never allowed pets. But," she looked around at the home she shared with her mother. "I can't leave everything here and I have school."

"You can bring whatever you need. It will give you some time to decide on what to do next. We can figure out how to get you to school. And, I can always use an extra hand around the place."

"I guess it would be okay for one night. It's been really hard being here alone, even though mom's friends have been stopping by constantly."

"Great, it's settled. We'll pack up a few things for tonight and we can come back tomorrow for whatever else you need."

The knots in my chest began to loosen with the knowledge that Jenny would be safe with Bailey. The reception didn't look like it was going to wrap up anytime soon but I needed to meet with the mayor's housekeeper. I was more determined than ever to find out who killed him. Leaving Bailey to work out the final details with Jenny, I went home to change for my visit to creepy housekeeper.

I had promised myself I would never return to the scene of his murder, but I would make this one last exception in the hope of wrapping a pretty ribbon around the case for my acquittal. As I gassed up the rental, my phone buzzed with a text message from a blocked number.

Jayne, help me. I'm hurt. At Rattlesnake Cove Bartlett Lake. Hurry. Me

The only person who ever sent me a message as "me" was Emmett. Why his number would show as blocked didn't make sense, but I didn't want to waste time figuring that out if he needed me. I jumped in the car and hurried toward the lake. I knew a little of the history of Bartlett Lake, but being somewhat adverse to water after my father's accident, I had never spent any time there.

Emmett, an exercise fanatic, had told me that the park bordered by the Verde River, was one of his favorite places. The river starts north of Phoenix and fills with monsoon rains and snowmelt as it winds its way south to the Salt River, didn't sound appealing to me. After passing through Carefree, I would have another twenty plus miles to the lake. On this same road, I escaped from the clutches of the mayor, and Jonas rescued me.

I floored the rental car thinking, as I paused briefly at the stop sign at Mule Train Road, to send Emmett a text to tell him I was on my way. He was an avid hiker and would bike for miles to get to a good walking trail. Still, I thought it strange he would have left to go hiking with the wind chasing black clouds across the sky.

It made me anxious when I didn't receive any

response back from him, but I could barely text while standing still, let alone driving. How would I ever find him on the trail? Hopefully he would be able to hear me calling his name and, if he were injured, I would be able to reach him without needing a helicopter.

During tourist season in the Valley of the Sun, mountain rescues routinely occurred when hikers slipped on the sometimes-dangerous trails. Out-of-towners would brave the mountains without sufficient water or any training, only to find Mother Nature wasn't kidding around. Even though Emmett was a finely tuned machine, accidents could happen to anyone. Perhaps he had been distracted watching an eagle fly overhead and had taken one small misstep, causing him to lose his footing and tumble down a steep slope. A million different scenarios ran through my head as I pushed the rental car even harder on the twisting road to hurry to his rescue. At last, I could finally do something good for someone else.

I flinched as a loud boom of thunder sounded directly overhead. The wind whipped around me and shook my car as if I were inside an industrial blender. Dust and sand slammed me from each side while tumbleweeds bounced off the windshield. On a clear day, I could have been easily navigated the hairpin turns but, with the wall of sand kicked up by the oncoming storm, I had difficulty seeing ten feet in front of the car. Each mile made me more desperate to reach Emmett. Being exposed in the middle of a haboob was like standing in front of a sand blaster. I turned on the headlights, praying no one slammed into the back of me, and hoping for the storm to pass quickly without the rain it promised.

Lightening flashed, striking the ground mere feet away, and the Arizona sky decided to dump a year's worth of water all at one time. It was an odd time of year for a storm, and a feeling of déjà vu rattled my brain. Each clap of thunder tightened my grip on the steering wheel. Subconsciously, I slowed, forcing my brain to focus on the moment and not get dragged back sixteen years. I couldn't relive that day again.

With my windshield wipers slapping time to the beats of my heart, I leaned closer to peer out. After driving for what seemed like hours, I finally saw the turnoff for Bartlett Lake Dam Road.

The desert drank the rain in giant thirsty gulps, but couldn't keep up with the pace of the torrent. The road rose ahead and currents of water raced toward me, digging trenches in the soft sand shoulders. Within a short distance, I could make out the sign indicating I was entering the Tonto National Forest. It seemed an odd name, since it wasn't what an East Coast girl would think of as a forest. This rugged region of the three-million-acre forest was part of the

Sonoran Desert studded with saguaro, cholla, hedgehog and prickly pear cactus. As far as I knew, there was only one Ranger Station in this part of the park and with rain battering me, I didn't expect to see any other hikers or tourists. It looked like I would be the only person fool enough to be heading to the lake on a day such as this.

The road twisted and turned, and dropped sharply as I hit the first of several washes. Camp Creek Wash had a small trickle of water running perpendicular to the road, but I knew it was only the beginning. I hoped we could make it back out before it became a wall of water. Arizona residents knew the most dangerous thing to do was to risk driving through a wash when a storm hit. It wasn't unusual for dry bed to become a raging current in a matter of minutes. Hitting the wash, I gunned the car, making sure to clear it as fast as I could.

Another earsplitting clap of thunder made the little car tremble. Lightening collided with the ground nearby while rain pummeled me from all sides. My hands hurt from gripping the steering wheel and my leg was cramping from alternating between the gas and brake. I held my breath as I saw a sign for the Indian Wells Wash ahead.

"Dad, I hope you're watching over me right now," I prayed.

I slowed to a stop as I approached the wash, trying to

peer out the windshield to see how much water was rushing by. It looked like I could make it, but I had to remember this wasn't a pickup truck and the rental didn't have much ground clearance. No choice but to keep going, so I stepped lightly on the gas to maintain my speed. I didn't want to risk splashing water up and stalling out the engine.

Making it safely to the other side, I exhaled and pushed down harder to pick up speed again. Images of Emmett hurt and lying on a bank while the water crept closer and closer to him spurred me on. I had to get to him before it was too late.

At last I could see a sign ahead welcoming me to the Bartlett Lake Recreation Area. My ears popped as I crested the last hill and started down towards the lake. As if on cue, the rain suddenly ceased and a lone ray of sun poked through the clouds, illuminating an island in the middle of the lake. Even from this distance I could see the water churning from the violence of the storm. From the top of the hill it looked as if I would drive right off the edge of the earth into the water.

I slowed down as I neared signs for the Jojoba Trail and the Yellow Cliffs boat launch. I kept going down to the lake watching for a sign for Rattlesnake Cove. The road turned to the left just before the main parking area and the Ranger Station. I wondered for a brief second if I should go to the Ranger Station to see if someone could help me, but ignored my common sense, figuring I could always go back for help if I needed it. Besides there was no car in the Ranger Station parking lot, so I figured that meant no ranger around either.

The road wound around to the right and I pulled into the first parking spot. I looked around for Emmett's car and not seeing it, I considered he might have been biking the trails instead of hiking. As I climbed out of the car, a large raindrop splatted on my face reminding me the storm was only taking a brief respite and would likely start up again in full force.

From the top parking area, I found a set of stairs leading down to a second parking lot, and I could see a row of picnic tables, each under its own ramada. I continued down another three sets of steps getting closer and closer to the lake's edge.

"Emmett! It's Jayne. Are you here?" I called out. The only answer was the sound of the wind as it whipped my hair into a mass of tangles.

I looked around to see where he could have gone and found a packed gravel trail heading off the main picnic area to the left. The hairs rose on the back of my neck and I glanced around me quickly. I hesitated but, on a mission, I gathered my courage and started walking along the path, calling his name as I went. After a short distance, I couldn't see the picnic area at all and the rain started again in full force. Darn him for deciding to hike when a storm was coming! My clothes were soaked in seconds, causing me to shiver from the temperature drop and wind.

The forceful downpour flowed over the high bank to my left creating a series of waterfalls. I grasped the handrail trying desperately to maintain my balance to keep from sliding down the rest of the way. Feeling more than seeing where I was headed, I could tell the path was making a sharp right turn.

"Jayne, down here." A voice called to me, carried by the wind from a distance.

"I'm coming." I yelled.

Another loud clap of thunder was followed immediately by a flash of lightning, which lit up the dark sky and allowed me to see a floating dock at the bottom of a long ramp. Beneath the metal roof, I could just make out the shape of a person in a hooded rain slicker waving madly to me. Another break in the storm gave me the opportunity to see the path. It dropped down at a forty-degree angle, guaranteeing a difficult descent. I held on to the rail and slip-slided my way down, hydroplaning in my worn flip-flops. Mentally berating myself for not stopping at the Ranger Station, I wondered how I would ever help Emmett back up the slope with the rain coming at us full force.

Almost to the dock, a strong blast of wind hit me in the face, knocking me backward. I landed hard on my rear end and skated the rest of the way down gathering more than a few splinters from the rough planks. My body slammed into the metal railing but, despite the collision, I was grateful it prevented me from plunging into the raging lake just a few feet below.

A hand reached out to help me up, but I recoiled. The ruby eyes of the rattlesnake ring glittered, the tail raised to give warning of an impending lethal strike.

"Tami Lynn, what are you doing here?" I asked unable to grasp what was really going on.

Tami Lynn cackled as she gazed down at me, "Jayne, I'm so happy you decided to drop in."

Pulling myself up, I looked around, "Where is Emmett?"

Shrugging her shoulders, she responded, "I haven't the slightest idea where your little friend is. You're here because we need to talk."

"You sent me the text," I said as the realization dawned on me. "I thought it was from my friend Emmett."

"You're not much of a challenge. A couple of hours of following you around and I know your entire life story. For someone who has been causing me so much trouble, you're a little slow on the uptake."

Glancing around, Tami Lynn reached into her jacket and pulled out a large handgun. "Now start walking, we're going to take a little trip."

Tami Lynn nudged me with the gun to the opposite side of the dock and down a few stairs to where a rowboat strained to break free. The wind continued to whip the lake into a fury while waves slammed the boat into the dock.

"Get in," she said, giving me a shove.

"A row boat? Seriously? I can't get in that!"

"It was the best I could do on short notice. Get in now, or I'll shoot you right here."

"I can't get in," I cried.

She gave me a hard shove and screamed, "Now!"

"If you're going to shoot me, do it here. I can't get in that boat. I would rather die here than on the water." I clung to the railing with an iron grip.

Tami Lynn held the gun to my head, "If you want to keep that cute boyfriend alive, you'll do as I say. Now get in the boat before the ranger figures out I sent him on a wild goose chase."

First Emmett, and now Jonas. I didn't know what Tami Lynn had done, but I had a strong feeling I knew what she was capable of doing. I stepped off the dock into the boat on trembling legs. The rain lessened to a drizzle as I took my seat and picked up the oars.

Tami Lynn untied the boat and stepped in behind me. "Now start rowing out to the island," she ordered, pointing with the gun toward the middle of the lake.

I picked up the oars and began to row. My heart threatened to jump out of my chest as waves splashed over the sides of the pint-sized boat and we rocked precariously from side to side. I felt the bile rise in my throat as my panic started.

Although the rain had taken another hiatus, the wind had not lessened, and it took all the strength I had to keep the boat from capsizing.

I panted with the effort of rowing. "Why?"

"Less chance someone will interrupt us out there. And stop worrying about why, just row."

I glanced around and saw no one in sight. There didn't seem to be much chance of anyone happening by on an afternoon hike in the middle of a monsoon-type storm. I kept my mouth shut on the rest of the journey, concentrating on keeping us afloat more than trying to put all of the pieces together.

It took me twenty minutes of huffing and puffing before my blistered hands ran us ashore on the far side of the island.

"She waved the gun at me and ordered me to pull the

boat up on shore.

I did as instructed and stepped into the icy cold water on my quivering legs. The slippery rocks almost caused me to lose my balance trying to drag the rowboat up onto shore. Once on solid ground again, I was able to finally take a breath and try to steady my nerves. It was impossible to tell if I was more frightened of Tami Lynn's gun or the water.

"Okay, we're here now. Can you tell me what is so important you had to risk our lives and wave a gun in my face?" My bravado was tainted by the quake in my voice.

"Start walking." Again she poked me with the gun and pointed in the direction she wanted me to head.

The storm was still on coffee break and even the winds seemed to have tapered off, at least for the moment. We scrambled up a bank, and she pointed me in the direction of a small three-sided shack where Bougainvillea clung with its tentacle-like arms, partially hiding the opening.

"Have a seat and make yourself at home. It's almost as neat and tidy as your place." She said chuckling to herself.

"*You* who broke into my apartment? Did you hurt my cat?"

"You're the one who needs to answer questions. Where is my money?"

"Wh-what money?" I stammered.

"You know what money. I know it's not in your

apartment or that hunk of junk you drive around."

"You're the lady seller! Now it makes sense—real estate agent by day, madam by night. Oh my God, you killed the mayor and Kiki and that poor boy, too. Why did you do it?"

Her mouth curled into a sneer. "I only did what I had to do. Franklin was a jerk. He suckered me in with all his promises, then stole my money and tried to blackmail me. Even after all of that, I believed he and I could do great things together, but he thought he could slap me around and get away with it." Tami Lynn waved the gun around as she became more agitated.

"But why murder him? Couldn't you just have gone your separate ways?"

"He stole a hundred grand from me and wanted more. I worked hard for my money and I wasn't planning to give it to him."

"He got the pictures you took of Trent. Is that what he was blackmailing you with?" I asked.

"No, those pictures were Franklin's idea. He needed to get Trent in line and I was happy to help. But then that stupid boy Jimmy started getting greedy and told his friend Kiki what was going on. Franklin stole a copy of my client list and was going to hit up all my clients or release their names to the press. It would have put me out of business. I couldn't allow that." Tami Lynn pulled a plastic baggie with a piece of paper out of her back pocket. "You just need to sign this little confession and I'll be on my way."

I needed to hold her off long enough to come up with a plan. My hands shook as I scrawled my name and handed my confession back to her. "Why frame me for his murder? What do you have against me?"

She laughed, sealing the confession in the plastic bag and stuffing it back in her pocket, "You were so easy. I didn't plan it to happen the night of the cocktail party but, when Franklin pulled his stunt, you became the perfect mark."

"How did you know I had the bag with the money?"

"Franklin told me he gave it to you that night. I searched his house twice, and your place, and couldn't find it."

"It must have been him that put the key in my apron. I figured out it was for a locker at the Scottsdale airport. I'll find a way to be sure the police track you down. I have the list, your money, and now your confession."

"You'll tell me where my client list and money are or you won't leave this island alive." Tami Lynn said, pulling back the hammer on the gun with a resounding click.

"If you kill me, you'll never get either."

"Listen, honey, you'll tell me where my stuff is if you know what's good for you and your friends. No one suspects me in any of those murders, and I'll make sure the cops find enough evidence to put you away forever."

"If I tell you where the money is, how do I know you won't kill me anyways?"

"She waved the gun in my face. You'll go to jail for Franklin's murder, or you'll die here alone on this island from what will look like a self-inflicted gunshot wound. It's your choice. I'm trying to be nice." She sneered at me.

"That's your idea of nice? I get a choice of a lifetime in prison or a gunshot to the head?"

"I'm happy either way. It would be easier if you would just tell me where my money is but, if not, this gun is my backup plan. I'll just use the confession as your suicide note."

My heart pounded so hard I thought my chest would explode. The wind whipped my hair in my eyes, and I knew time was running out. I had to either tell her where the money was or take my chances with the gun. I wasn't convinced she wouldn't shoot me just for the pure fun of it.

"Bailey, Emmett, and Jonas know I'm innocent."

"That's your problem. Either convince them you did it, or put their lives in jeopardy, too. Funny thing about murder, once you've done it, each one gets a little easier," Tami Lynn said, shrugging her shoulders. "Would be a shame to have to dispose of a few bodies before I leave town, but it can be arranged."

Just then, something my father had told me many years ago, flashed through my mind. When I asked him how he handled criminals when there was the possibility of a shootout, he told me, "You get one chance. There's a split second when you have to make a decision whether it's going to be him or you. You have to grab the chance before it passes by, then live with your choice." This was it for me. I had to go for the gun because my gut told me there would be no prison term for me. Once she knew where the money was, I would be dead by suicide, and the note she forced me to sign would be my last words.

"Okay, you win. I'll draw you a map to where I hid the bag with your money and client list." My hand shook violently as I held it out to her, hoping she would dig in her pocket for the only paper she had—my confession.

Tami Lynn lowered the gun slightly, providing my split second of opportunity. I slammed into her, throwing my shoulder into her arm. The gun flew out of her hand as we both collapsed on the wet ground. She scratched my face with her claw-like fingernails as I tried to get a grip on her.

Pushing me off her with strength I wouldn't have guessed she had, she crawled towards the gun.

"Not if I get there first!" I yelled, scurrying on my hands and knees after her.

We both reached the gun at the same time and the melee began anew. We rolled over and over, both of us trying to gain control of the weapon, sliding down the embankment. For once it was my mother's voice ringing in my head, "Fight, Jayne, fight!" she yelled. Or, maybe it was me yelling but, either way, I wasn't going to let a crazy woman have another chance to kill me.

Two sets of hands held the gun as a bullet exploded from the barrel. We both froze, staring into each other's eyes. I wondered why I wasn't in pain, but maybe I was too far in shock to feel anything. Releasing my grip on the gun, I rolled away from Tami, looking down at myself to see where I had been shot. There was no blood except on my hands. I looked at Tami clutching her stomach as blood ran between her fingers. The gun lay on the ground between us.

"You shot me!" she screamed as thunder cracked and the sky dumped another deluge of water.

"Oh my God, I shot you!"

"Get me to a hospital, you idiot."

Wiping the rain from my face, I stood and looked around. We needed help, but no one could see us from the Ranger Station, even if anyone was there. My phone was in my car. No one knew where we were, and Tami Lynn would likely bleed out before I could row us back across the lake. I looked at her, then out at the water, which churned maliciously. No way could I row us back. The wind was now blasting us with sand, and rain coming in sideways, beating my face like a thousand pin pricks. The last thing I wanted was to escape from one dangerous situation into another. It would be suicide to get in the tiny boat with the waves now cresting over three feet. The boat would capsize and we would drown. We had no life jackets in this vessel. It was us against mother nature and I didn't like our odds.

I glanced at Tami Lynn, deathly pale and shivering. Blood soaked the front of her designer blouse and her eyes were closed. She may have been a murderer, but I couldn't let her die. Besides she was the proof of my innocence.

"Tami Lynn, can you hear me? I need you to help me get you into the boat." I yelled over the rain as it pummeled us.

Her eyes flickered open for a second and a moan escaped her lips. I would have to do this on my own. I had to stop the bleeding, so I tugged off my soaking wet pants and tied them around her waist. I pulled her up to a sitting position and half dragged, half carried her down the bank to the boat. I somehow heaped her into the bottom of the boat and pushed with all my strength to get it back in the water. The sandy soil had turned into a mess of quicksand and my steps buried me almost up to the knees.

"Come on, Jayne, you can do this. You *have* to do

this," I screamed to myself.

I took a deep breath and gave one final shove with all of the strength I possessed. The boat launched, and I scrambled in before Tami Lynn sailed off without me. I grabbed the oars and started rowing with all my might. Waves breached the sides of the small boat as we tossed from side to side. I tried to row downwind to avoid surfing a wave, which could potentially bury the bow in the wave ahead. If that happened, we would surely capsize.

I rowed for all I was worth, praying to all the powers that be we would make it to the Ranger Station. For every few feet we moved in the direction I aimed, we were pushed back half as far. I promised to be a better person, have more patience, do charity work, clean my apartment regularly, call my mother more often, and stop cussing. I think I'd made these same promises a lot lately, to no avail. This time I hoped someone heard me.

"Come on, Tami Lynn, hang in there. We're almost back!" I yelled every few strokes to make sure she didn't die on me before I could turn her over to the police.

The small boat rose up with each new wave and I almost lost it a few times, but sheer determination kept me going. I would not lose another person in a storm. She was a murderess and hadn't given poor Kiki a chance to make a better life for her daughter, but I wouldn't have her death on my conscience. I had lived too many years hating myself for failing to save my father. I couldn't and wouldn't add another person to my guilt.

Despite my force of will, the rowboat was no match for the wind gusts and high waves. I could see the shore in sight but, before I could propel us the last fifty yards, another wave hit and we somersaulted over, dumping both Tami Lynn and me into the cold water.

On automatic pilot, I came up for air and starting searching for her. She wouldn't have been thrown far from the boat, and I knew, in her semi-conscious state, she would drown in a matter of seconds. I ducked under the water again, feeling for her as I swam. Rising to the surface, lightening flashed and I glimpsed her body floating face-down only feet from my grasp, next to the boat. I kicked as hard as I could to reach her before the next wave carried her out of my reach. Grabbing her around the neck, I flipped her over face up. She coughed and cried out in pain. I seized the side of the boat with one hand, but it was slick and my fingers numb. I couldn't just hang on and hope we washed ashore in time to save Tami Lynn. It was swim for shore or sink.

Swimming on my back as I pulled Tami Lynn with me, it felt like another hour of fighting the elements. Finally, when I felt I wouldn't make it and was ready to give up, my feet kicked against the lake bottom. I staggered to the shore, dragging her along with me to safety. I couldn't see how far it was to the Ranger Station. She needed an ambulance. Her skin felt ice cold as I checked for a pulse. It was there, but faint, and she had lost a lot of blood.

"I have to leave you here for just a few minutes so I can get help. Open your eyes, can you hear me?" I asked, shaking her.

Her eyes flickered open for a second and she coughed up more of the lake water. It wasn't the best place to leave her, but she was far enough on shore the waves wouldn't drag her back out. As lightening flashed again, I made out the shape of a building and headed in that direction.

Running in sand is hard even when it's not in the middle of a torrential rainstorm, but I had no choice. I moved with labored steps in slow motion towards where I had seen the building, hoping I could get help in time. I paused between steps to remember where I was going as my brain started to shut down from the cold seeping into my bones.

Light shone from the station windows and I made out the shape of cars in the parking lot. Gasping for breath, I crawled on my hands and knees up the stairs to the Ranger Station. I pulled myself up and clawed open the door, flinging myself on the first person I saw, who happened to be Jonas. Putting aside my shock, I rattled off instructions about where to find Tami Lynn and, in a heartbeat, Jonas and the ranger dashed out the door. The last thing I remember hearing was the scream of sirens as I let the exhaustion and fear take over and slid slowly to the floor.

CHAPTER EIGHTEEN

"I'm so glad we got here when we did," said Bailey, as she crouched beside me on the floor, wrapping a scratchy blanket around my shoulders.

My body shook convulsively and my teeth clattered together so hard I could barely form words. "How?" I asked her.

"You sent Emmett an odd text saying you were on your way. He knew something was wrong and, when you didn't answer your cell, he called me. I called Jonas and he hadn't heard from you either."

"Find me?"

"Let's just say I got a little creative and maybe *accidentally* found my way into the rental car's satellite tracking system. When it showed the car was here at the lake, I called

Ben." Bailey tucked the blanket around me more tightly, trying to stop the shivering.

I could hear the sound of sirens nearing. "Tami Lynn?"

"When we arrived in the storm and saw your car, but couldn't find you, the ranger called for backup and an ambulance. They should be here any minute."

I could hear the sound of voices and frenetic activity outside the Ranger Station while the wailing wind rattled the windows and the rain ran off the roof like the blood between Tami Lynn's fingers. Minutes may have passed or hours, I couldn't tell.

The door flung open and Jonas rushed in. He knelt beside me. "Are you hurt?"

I shook my head no, but my shivering was becoming more violent, and I wanted nothing more than to close my eyes and sleep. "C-c-cold," I chattered.

"She may have hypothermia and be going into shock. That water is cold enough, if she was in it for longer than thirty minutes, we could have a serious problem. We need to get her to the hospital, but the washes are flooding and I'm not sure another vehicle will make it," the ranger said as he peered at me over Jonas' shoulder.

"My truck will make it if we leave right now." Jonas swept me up in his arms and ran out the door with Bailey on his heels.

"It's too risky to go back out in this storm!" The ranger called after us, to no avail.

"Bailey, you stay here," Jonas ordered her.

"Not on your life, buddy. Where she goes, I go."

Jonas unceremoniously dumped me in the crew cab of his truck and, with Bailey riding shotgun, we blasted out of the parking lot. I'd heard the ambulance leaving with Tami Lynn moments before and, if we didn't come across them on the way, at least I would know she made it to the hospital before the washes flooded too much to cross.

I lay on the back seat hugging the blanket, too worn out to mind the distinct smell of wet dog. Closing my eyes, I fell into a dream-like trance. I thought this must be Molly's blanket. I wonder where Bugsy is right now and if he misses me. I thought I heard my mother talking to someone on the phone, and then I felt like a passenger on a fast-moving train rushing past a station.

"We need to stop at the station and get Bugsy. His suitcases are all packed." I said to my mother.

"Bugsy doesn't need his suitcases. He has whatever he needs at home. It's going to be okay, Jayney. Mom is here now."

I felt someone softly stroking my forehead and singing a lullaby remembered from my childhood. I appreciated the reassuring sensations and drifted back into my lovely dreams.

When I awoke, I lay in a hospital bed, surrounded by a garden of flowers and the soft sound of my mother's voice.

"Mom?" I whispered through a raw and scratchy throat.

"Oh, honey, you're awake. I'm here." My mother had been talking quietly on her cell phone. Saying a quick goodbye, she came to my bedside. "You gave us all quite a scare," she said kissing my cheek.

"What happened? Am I at home?" I croaked, wondering if this is what Dorothy had felt like in *The Wizard of Oz*.

"You're in the hospital. You had hypothermia and we were worried we were going to lose you." Her voice cracked, and she coughed to try to cover a sob.

Shadowy memories started creeping into my still foggy brain. "Tami Lynn? Is she alive?"

"Yes, she made it through surgery." My mother held a plastic cup with a straw up to my mouth. "Here take a small drink, it will help your throat."

I sipped quietly for a few seconds, trying to sort through what I remembered and what I may have imagined. I gave an involuntary shudder as I recalled battling the storm and the icy cold permeating my body.

The door to my room opened and, as a nurse walked in, I glimpsed a Sheriff's deputy posted outside my door.

"Oh my God, am I under arrest?" I rasped.

My mother patted my hand, "He's here for your protection."

I waited for the nurse to check my vital signs, again mentally tallying up the cost of this visit and its effect on my bank account before I summoned the courage to ask, "My protection?"

"From that vile woman, Tami Lynn Carroll. I would like to get my hands on her."

Before I could pump her for more details, the door opened with a loud swoosh and in strode Jonas. Obviously, he and my mother had met, but I still felt uncomfortable and underdressed.

"Hey there, darlin'. Nice to see you've come back to us," Jonas said as he leaned down and kissed my forehead.

The nurse checked one of the monitors. "We'll have to get you up and moving around as soon as possible. Do you feel like taking a walk down the hall?"

"I think it's too soon for her to get up," my mother said, folding her arms across her chest. I could see the mother bear coming out, and figured I better intervene.

"I can get up. I don't want to stay in here any longer than necessary."

"We need you up so fluid doesn't settle in your lungs. I'll have an orderly come assist you."

"That's not necessary. I can walk with her," Jonas volunteered.

My mother shook her head as if she was ready to argue, but gave in when Jonas assured her he wouldn't let me overexert myself.

"I guess I'll grab a cup of coffee while you take your walk." Keep an eye on our girl and keep her out of trouble. If you can, that is." My mother picked up her purse, gave me another kiss on the cheek, and was out the door.

Jonas helped me sit up and, between him and the nurse, got me situated with IV and heart-rate monitor.

When the nurse was sure I could stand with Jonas' support, she left. I grimaced up at his face. "This is really weird. "When did you and my mom become best friends?"

"Your mom is a special lady and she hasn't left this room since she got here."

"Maybe you could fill me in on what happened while I was out of it. The last thing I remember, we were heading out from the lake."

Jonas wrapped his arm tightly around me as we made a slow trip down the hall. "The ambulance made it out of Bartlett before the washes were impassable. We didn't do as well. Those few minutes from the time they left until I got you in the truck made five feet of difference in the water level. We made it through the first wash, but by the time we got to the Indian Wells wash, the current was too strong to chance it."

I shuddered as the memories crept back. I breathed in the smell of his aftershave and leaned against his strong arm.

"You were as white as a sheet and had stopped making any sense the first mile into the trip. You kept talking about Molly's blanket and Bugsy, and something about riding in trains. We turned around to go back to the Ranger Station, but were caught in the middle."

We shuffled to the end of the hallway and I paused to catch my breath. The effort of moving my legs was exhausting.

Jonas continued, "We had to ride out the storm in the truck until the water level went down enough to get you out. We got you out of the wet clothes but, even with the heater blasting, we couldn't get you to stop shivering."

I could see the memory of that moment expressed in the lines on his face which I was sure hadn't been there a few days earlier.

"We were stuck there for about an hour before the rain stopped and the water level dropped enough for me to risk driving through. By the time we got you here to the hospital, you were pretty out of it and, to be honest, I was scared you weren't going to make it. Bailey called your mother and she flew out the same night. She hasn't left your side in two days.

"I've been out for two days?"

"Part of it was doctor induced. They didn't want to bring you around too quickly, and had to raise your body temperature slowly. There was the risk of brain damage so..."

Only my sore throat kept me from shouting. Instead, all I could muster was a raspy "I have brain damage?" The beeping of the machine hooked to the cable running from my finger grew louder and more rapid to keep pace with the beating of my heart.

"Calm down, I was trying to say there was a risk, but it didn't happen. You're obviously back to your old self. Once the doctors took you off the drugs, we knew you would be okay. Then Tami Lynn disappeared from her hospital room and all hell broke loose around here."

We headed back to my room walking more slowly.

"Tami Lynn is missing? My mother said she had surgery. Where did she go?"

"The cops want to know that, too. We were able to piece together a lot of what happened from your ramblings in the truck, some from calling Kiki's daughter, and later we found your so-called confession in her pocket. Since it was typed, and sealed in a plastic bag, it was obviously a set up.

She was going to be charged with three murders and the attempt on your life, but somebody must have helped her escape before the cops could post a guard on her door. Your mother insisted they protect you in case she tried to come back and finish you off."

"There was so much blood. How could she have survived?"

"You saved her life. From what I heard, the bullet went through soft tissue and it looked worse than it was, but if you had left her on that island she would have bled out. You could have let her drown in the lake. Instead you almost got your crazy self killed trying to save her."

"I couldn't leave her to die." I shuddered at the memory of my struggle to get both of us back to shore alive.

"Now, she's on the run. I only hope she is far away and doesn't plan to return any time soon. The Sheriff's Department has been waiting to question you for the full story of what happened on the lake. The good news is the charges against you have been dropped. You can go home as soon as you're released."

My shoulders relaxed for the first time since my arrest. "What a relief."

"I think Detective Stewart got his rear end handed to him on a platter for messing up the investigation."

"Is Kiki's daughter okay?"

"Bailey can fill you in on that when she gets here. She had a few stops to make, but I expect she'll come waltzing in here soon. You know if she hadn't hacked into the rental car company records we may not have found you in time. She should work for the FBI," Jonas said with a touch of admiration in his voice.

The hallway seemed to have doubled in length, but we were finally back to my room. My legs wobbled a bit, but it felt good to have the strong arm of Jonas holding me up. My mind skipped to an image of him caring for me in his truck.

"Back up a minute there, cowboy. What was that part about getting me naked?"

"Jonas smiled, "It was for medical reasons only, I promise. I'd prefer to get you naked for other reasons."

"So I was medically naked on the backseat of your pickup truck. This would only happen to me." I could feel the embarrassment creeping up my checks.

Before we could pursue the conversation any further, Bailey and my mother strolled down the hall arm in arm.

"You all seem to be enjoying my misery a little too much," I said wearily as Jonas helped me back into bed.

All three heads nodded in unison.

CHAPTER NINETEEN

"You're being released this afternoon," my mother announced the next day.

I believed it was entirely due to my constant protestations about the cost of hospitalization, which finally wore down the staff. Whatever the reason, I was more than ready to get back to my little apartment and try to get my life on track.

My entourage of Jonas, Bailey, Emmett and my mother made sure I was safely snuggled in my bed with pillows fluffed and snacks nearby. It wasn't the same without Bugsy there with me, but I was starting to accept he might never return.

"Emmett is taking me to the airport this afternoon," my mother announced. "I've got some things I need to get back to at home."

"Mom, I'm sorry you had to come all the way out here to take care of me. The one constant is that I seem to keep screwing up my life."

"Jayne, when my girl almost dies, where else would I be? I wish you had told me about what was going on with that terrible Franklin person. Maybe I haven't made you feel you could confide in me, but you've always been such a survivor, I suppose I thought you didn't really need me."

"I thought you blamed me for Dad's death," I murmured uncomfortable saying the words out loud.

"I never blamed you for your father's death. I was angry with him for dying, and I was angry that he almost took you with him, but I never held you responsible. You were just a child, and I was so traumatized by it... I think maybe I was afraid to talk to you about it."

"I've always been such a screw-up and never seem to get anything right. I know I'm a disappointment to you."

"Whatever gave you that idea? I'll admit it was hard on me to stay strong when you moved to Arizona. I worry because you live so far away, but I understand you needed a fresh start, someplace to distance yourself from the memories. You have the courage to take chances, and sometimes in life it works out and sometimes it doesn't. I've always been proud of you."

I hugged my mother tight and knew we finally shared the mother/daughter. talk we should have had many years before. I admitted to myself, though, I hadn't been ready for it until now. Just before she left to fly home, she whispered she had met a really nice man and they were dating. I was overjoyed for her and, because of her, felt like a weight had been lifted from my shoulders.

As Jonas and I walked back to my apartment having said goodbye to my mother, I glanced over at my neighbor's apartment. Again, I saw the eyes staring back at me, and also a little pink nose twitching a hello.

"Jonas, look, I swear that's Bugsy in the window," I said, grabbing his arm and dragging him to the neighbor's door.

As we neared, I was convinced the nice little lady I met the first day I put out the lost cat flyers had catnapped Bugsy. There he sat in her window just as fat and happy as ever.

I banged on her door, prepared to break it down if I had to.

"Open up! I know you have my cat in there," I shouted as I beat my fists on the door.

I heard the chain being removed, and there she stood in all her polyester splendor.

"You may as well come in before someone calls the

police," she said. The door opened and she waved us in.

My beloved cat wrapped himself around my legs. He looked no worse for his long time away from me. In fact, he seemed to have gained a few pounds around the mid-section.

I swooped him up and covered his little face with kisses. "I've missed you so much, but I'm here to rescue you now," I said as he purred a throaty hello in return.

Jonas tapped my shoulder, pulling me out of my kitty love fest. "Jayne, I don't think he really needs to be rescued. Looks to me like the guy has been living the high life."

I looked around the room. Cat toys littered the floor, the wall on the far end of the room had a brand new six-foot kitty condo with levels for easy climbing, and the window had a plush leopard print seat for his highness to watch the birds. He had gone from downtown to uptown.

She rung her birdlike hands and tears filled her eyes. "I'm truly sorry I kept him. He wandered into my backyard and he was so sweet and lovable I couldn't resist. At first I thought he must have had a terrible owner to let him wander off, but when I met you that day I promised myself I would bring him home. Before I could, I saw you on the news accused of murder, and I figured you wouldn't be able to take care of Leonard so I would keep him."

"Leonard, who is Leonard?" I asked.

"That's what I call him. Named after my husband of

sixty years."

My Bugsy had become a Leonard, and the sad thing was he didn't even mind. He seemed happy with Arlene, and she obviously doted on him. But I loved him, too, and I wasn't ready to let him go.

"Jayne, can I see you outside for a minute?" Jonas asked softly as he pulled Bugsy from my arms.

"Jonas, if you ever think of seeing me again you will not suggest I leave my cat with her," I spat.

"How about a small compromise?"

In the end, it all worked out perfectly for me, Arlene and of course Bugsy, who got the best of the deal. Arlene would keep Bugsy at night while I worked, but in the morning she would drop him off to me when she took her walk. I would have him all day until I left for work when I would drop him back at her house for the night. She wouldn't be alone anymore, I would still have my best friend—four-legged anyways—and Bugsy would have love twenty-four seven, which he didn't mind at all.

The last task for me was to figure out what to do with Tami Lynn's money and client list. Since the police didn't know about the money, I figured I could put it to better use setting up a college fund for Kiki's daughter, Jenny. Bailey worked out the details so she would be her foster mother for a few short months, until Jenny graduated high school and left for college. I suppose, to Bailey, rescuing a kid wasn't much different than rescuing animals, and one more body in her home didn't bother her in the least.

The client list was mailed to the State Police anonymously, and I heard the indictments for a multitude of crimes besides prostitution would come about soon.

Tami Lynn remained on the loose, and I never did talk to the housekeeper again or her daughter, but it didn't seem to matter anymore.

Jonas and I made plans for another date. This time we were going out to dinner—just to be safe—since our last two attempts to eat in hadn't worked out too well.

Peter welcomed me back to the restaurant and was thrilled at my celebrity, which brought in a few new guests. I'm just glad to be back with my restaurant family, trading jabs with Emmett. My poor old Betsy was fixed enough to keep driving me to work, but I'm not making any bets on how long that will last.

My only remaining guilt was that I never did pay back the one thousand dollars borrowed from the money bag. Okay, so maybe it was actually five thousand, but that's another story.

ABOUT THE AUTHOR

Menu for Murder is Leslie Keller's debut novel. When not writing the next book in the series, or hiking in the desert, she can be found enjoying a glass of wine with some chocolate. Leslie lives in Arizona with her partner, Raymond and their two rescue cats, Magic and Chance.

Sign up through her website for book news at: www.lesliekellerbooks.com
Contact Leslie on Facebook at: www.facebook.com/lesliekellerbooks
Follow her on Twitter: https://twitter.com/leskellerbooks